MOMENT OF TRUTH

Martine was talking in a low voice, almost as if to herself. "When I was your age, Toni, I could hardly wait to get away from home. It was so awful."

What did she mean? What was she talking about? What was so awful?

"I don't understand," Toni said. "I don't know what you're talking about."

"Nothing," she said. "If you don't know…"

"If I don't know what?"

"They've kept you in ignorance," she said. "Leave it alone, Toni."

"I hate being treated like a dumb kid. Tell me what you mean!"

"Do you really want to know?" Martine said.

"Yes," Toni said, and her heart began that awful thumping.

The next moments she would remember forever…

Other Avon Flare Books by
Norma Fox Mazer

AFTER THE RAIN
DOWNTOWN
MRS. FISH, APE, AND ME, THE DUMP QUEEN
SILVER
TAKING TERRI MUELLER

NORMA FOX MAZER

Babyface

AVON BOOKS
A division of
The Hearst Corporation
1350 Avenue of the Americas
New York, New York 10019

Published by arrangement with the author
Library of Congress Catalog Card Number: 90-6485
ISBN: 0-380-75720-6
RL : 5.0

Published in hardcover by William Morrow and Company, Inc.; for information address Permissions Department, William Morrow and Company, Inc., 1350 Avenue of the Americas, New York, New York 10019.

First Avon Flare Printing: August 1991

Printed in Canada.

UNV 10 9 8 7 6

FOR
ELEANOR CLYMER

Babyface

FEATURE REPORT:

Best Friends Reassuring Tradition

by Patricia Abish

In this day and age, when so many cherished traditions have disappeared and parents wonder what bizarre fad their kids will come home with tomorrow, this reporter found that tradition lives reassuringly on in the persons of two teen girls, Julie Jensen and Toni Chessmore. Julie and Toni live next door to each other and are best friends. "It was our destiny," says Toni with a charming giggle.

Fifteen years ago Julie's and Toni's parents each bought their first homes, modest three-bedroom houses on Oak Street. Steven and Jerrine Jensen each had a business: Steven dealt in paint supplies; Jerrine was involved with building her cosmetics line. Next door, Harold Chessmore was a dedicated fireman, while Violet Chessmore managed a drugstore. The two young couples were strangers, but their shared ideals and ambitions quickly made them friends. They had even more in common when the baby girls, Toni and Julie, were born the following year.

Toni is a younger sister, Julie an older sister. "As you can see, otherwise we're just alike," quips Julie, a tall, classic blue-eyed blonde, contrasting strongly to Toni, a slight, dark-haired girl with enormous brown eyes. Their birthdays in May are only a week apart. "Big important week," says Toni. "Right," says Julie with a grin. "I'm older, so that makes me wiser."

The two girls call each other first thing in the morning (on the phone or out the window, depending on the weather), do their homework together, and spend their weekends and holidays together. Now on spring vacation, they have been helping a temporarily incapacitated neighbor, visiting her daily to clean, shop, and do small chores. Do they mind washing dishes? "No," laughs Julie. "It's fun to do anything, as long as we do it together." They look at each other and nod. "We like to keep busy!"

This reporter couldn't help feeling that in these girls and their friendship and their families, the best of old-fashioned American traditions persist.

• CHAPTER •
ONE

Toni had always thought of herself as lucky. Toni Luck, she called it. She was lucky in her parents, lucky to have Julie. Those were the big things. But what about the little things, like the way Paws had come to her, just showed up at their house one day and stayed? Pure luck. Or how about the way she was always finding money in the street? Usually it was only a quarter or a dime, but once she had found a ten-dollar bill, and another time a silver dollar. Julie said Toni was probably the only kid in the world who could take a casual walk anywhere and pick up her allowance on the way.

Toni's lucky feeling about herself was why she wasn't even that surprised when a reporter from the *Ridgewood Record* wanted to write a story about her and Julie. Julie was the one who got excited. "This could be important. What if a Hollywood producer sees my picture—"

"Julie, I really don't think they read the *Record* in Hollywood," Toni said.

"But what if one did and saw me and thought, 'By Jove, that girl is photogenic and has talent!' "

"Don't think they say 'by Jove,' either, Jul."

"Shut up, Toni."

"Whatever you say, Julie."

The *Ridgewood Record* came out once a week with news and articles about people in their town. Small-town paper, only about eight pages and filled with ads, the features squeezed in between. How the paper happened to run the article about her and Julie was, Toni thought, like a Rube Goldberg contraption. The kind of thing where you press a button and a window flies open, which hits someone in the head, who falls down and knocks over a chair, which breaks a dish, which wakes the baby, who bites the dog.

The button in this case was Mrs. Abish, a widow who lived across the street at 92 Oak. One Sunday morning she got a yen for pancakes and noticed she didn't have any maple syrup. She got on her three-speed bike and rode over to Paulsons' Market, a mom-and-pop store on Poplar Avenue that was open from seven in the morning to midnight, seven days a week. Mr. Paulson happened to be in bed with a cold that day, so Mrs. Paulson was unusually busy, which was why she didn't know someone had broken a bottle of syrup right at the end of aisle three. Which was why Mrs. Abish, coming around the corner, walked right into the sticky mess, slipped, and went flat on her back.

"It must have been a glorious sight, me flailin' around on the floor like a fat fish," she said to anyone who would listen. Really she wasn't fat so much as large, or what Toni's mother kindly called well-padded. "Look at me. I used to be a slip of a girl. I'm this way from the grand food in this country," Mrs. Abish would say. She had been born in Ireland and rolled her *r*'s wonderfully.

She came home from the hospital with her leg in a cast. It was the beginning of spring vacation for Julie and Toni, and they didn't have that much to do, so they started going across the street to see if they could help Mrs. Abish, run to the store for her, or whatever. (Actually it had been Toni's mother's idea to begin with.)

Mrs. Abish was delighted. "Is that you, loves?" she'd call when she heard their steps on the porch. Inside, she'd be sitting on the couch with her leg extended on a stool. Toni and Julie would sit down and talk to her for a while, then they'd dust or wash the dishes, whatever she wanted done. One day toward the end of vacation, when they went over, Mrs. Abish's niece was visiting. Patricia Abish was a reporter, and Mrs. Abish had told her all about Julie and Toni. That was the beginning of the article. They were interviewed, they were photographed, everything very professional.

The day the story appeared, Julie read the article out loud, with appropriate gestures. "In this day and age, when so *many*"—arms spread wide—"*cherished*"—hand to heart—"traditions have *disappeared*"—hand over eye, peering into the distance—"and parents wonder . . ."

They spread the newspaper out on the floor and checked out the pictures. "You can hardly see me," Toni said. In every picture (there were three) she was looking down, looking away, or more or less hanging out behind Julie. Not great, but she wasn't photogenic like Julie.

"My lips are sticking out," Julie said. "Look at them, they poke out. Do they always stick out like that?"

"Julie, your lips are beautiful. You've got full lips."

Julie stared at herself in the mirror, front face, then at

each profile. "I might have to have my lips fixed, like that ballet dancer, Gelsey Kirkland. She got herself full lips. I'll get mine cut down."

"Julie, ugh! Sick. Don't ever do anything like that."

"Oh, I couldn't, anyway, it costs a huge amount of money. You have to be rich."

Toni's parents bought a dozen extra copies of the newspaper. Her mother clipped the article and sent it to everyone: to Toni's sister, Martine, in New York City; to her uncle in Paris; to her grandmother in Los Angeles. Her father framed a copy for the family room. He laminated another copy and took it with him to the fire station. The last time he'd tacked an article on the bulletin board there had been three years ago when the *Record* had run a feature titled "Men as Cooks." They'd printed Toni's father's picture and his recipe for Pizza-in-a-Hurry.

For a while it seemed as if Toni couldn't go anywhere in the neighborhood without someone saying, "I saw your picture in the paper." A kid she didn't even know passed her and Julie on his bike and yelled, "I read about you two!" Mrs. Frankowitz, who lived in the corner house, stopped Toni to say she'd had an article written about her once, too. "I was even younger than you. I won a gymnastic competition," she said, smiling, showing tiny gray teeth.

What made it all even more embarrassing was that Patricia Abish had gotten so many things wrong. For instance, Toni's mother wasn't manager of Rite Bargain Drugs, she was *assistant* manager. Julie's father was a salesman, not a businessman. And Mrs. Jensen hadn't even started her door-to-door cosmetics business until a year ago. Little details like that.

There were other things, too. She'd written that Toni and Julie's parents were good friends, but really, it was more in the line of good neighbors who got together once or twice a year for a barbecue in the backyard. And Toni wished she only *were* slight. That sounded a lot better to her than skinny. Gaining weight was a big struggle. She had these elbows and knees—pointy, bony things. Julie said she could always use them as weapons in hand-to-hand combat.

Patricia Abish did get Julie right, tagging her as blond and blue-eyed, except that sounded so bland, so vanilla pudding. Exactly what Julie wasn't.

"What bugs me," Julie said, "is that I never said you and I were alike."

"I think she was being ironic, Jul," Toni said.

"Whatever," Julie said. "I could list a hundred differences. Starting with cats." Julie tolerated Paws for Toni's sake. "But I don't forget that he's one of the sneaky tribe," she always said. "He'll lick your hand, then go out and kill an innocent bird."

"It's cat nature to hunt," Toni said. "They don't do it to be cruel. They don't have a concept of cruelty. That's human beings." Paws leaped up on Toni's lap. He was always a little skittery around Julie, but Toni still kept trying to bring the two of them together.

"Want to hold him, Jul?" She cuddled Paws. He was a small, cream-streaked-with-chocolate cat, some Siamese in his ancestry somewhere. "When people play with pets, their heartbeat slows down and it calms them."

"My heartbeat can slow down when I get old, Toni."

"You're missing a lot. A cat is a friend forever."

"Calling Hallmark Cards! Spare me the slop. I do not need a four-legged slimeball killer for a friend, Toni."

Toni kissed Paws's little heart-shaped face and whispered in his ear not to mind Julie. She was used to Julie's harangues. It was part of the way they balanced each other: Toni was dark, Julie blond. Toni was slight, Julie not. Toni was shy, Julie outspoken. *That* really was their biggest difference.

• CHAPTER • TWO

A new boy enrolled in school. Julie made it her business to find out about him, but nobody knew much. All Julie knew was his name, L.R. Faberman, and that he always wore black T-shirts and sunglasses. And he was strong. "He does the pegboard every day at lunchtime in the gym," she told Toni. She pointed him out in the hall. "Look interesting?"

"Cute," Toni said.

"I could fall in love with him," Julie said.

In the girls' room, Toni sat on a sink watching Julie putting on makeup. Julie was expert. She'd been doing it for years. She dusted on blusher, outlined her lips with a pencil, and filled in with lipstick. A layer of lip gloss over that, then another layer of lipstick. The cosmetics were samples from her mother. Makeup looked good on Julie. She had the cheeks for it, and those full lips she objected to.

Julie took a cigarette out of her purse, stuck it in the corner of her mouth, and lit up. "How does this look, Toni?"

"It looks like if your mother knew, she'd hang you from the ceiling by your thumbs."

"She smokes plenty, so she should say nothing." Julie held the cigarette in the middle of her mouth between her thumb and forefinger. "I'm doing this for professional reasons. When I have to play a character who smokes, I'll be ready. Lots of plays and movies have smoking in them." She switched the cigarette to the corner of her mouth again.

"Don't inhale," Toni warned.

"Don't worry, I don't plan to become a smoking maniac like your father."

Toni held out her hand. "Let me try."

"Uh-uh!" Julie jumped back. "I would never let you smoke!"

"Hey, girl, you're doing it."

"You're not me. You're too innocent. And younger."

"Julie, one stupid little week doesn't make me younger."

Julie puffed at the cigarette, watching herself in the mirror. "Swear you won't tell. If Heather found out, she'd squeal to Mom like a pig."

"I'm insulted. I would not say a word to Heather."

"Do I hear my name?" Heather said, walking in.

Julie put the cigarette behind her back. Toni palmed it and went into one of the stalls.

"What are you two talking about now?" Heather said. She was ten months younger than Julie. She had her own friends but always seemed irritated by Julie and Toni's closeness.

"Nothing that would interest you," Julie said.

"I heard them announce your birthday this morning, Toni," Heather called.

"I know." Toni flushed away the cigarette. "It was a mistake."

"What a bunch of jerks," Heather said. "Two weeks early."

Toni came out of the stall and washed her hands. Just thinking of the announcement this morning—"And we all want to wish Toni Chessmore a wonderful Happy Birthday!"—brought heat to her cheeks. Exactly the kind of thing she hated: everyone in the class looking at her.

Julie was bent over a sink, rinsing out her mouth.

"They better not goof with my birthday," Heather said. She brushed and rebraided her hair, which was thick and blond like Julie's. "They either get it right or I raise hell. I wish my birthday was right now. I love hearing my name called over the PA."

"You love anything about yourself," Julie said, packing away her cosmetics.

Heather flipped her braid at her sister. "And nothing about you." She inspected her teeth, smiled at herself approvingly, and pulled her T-shirt tight. "I've got more than either of you."

"If I stuffed my bra with socks, I'd have more, too," Julie said.

Heather smiled, but on the way out she turned to say, "Oh, Toni, is it true that the boys call you Toni Chess*less?*"

"Witch with a *B!*" Julie called after her sister.

Toni stared at herself in the mirror. Pearl earrings, blue work shirt, long full skirt, wavy crinkly hair falling around her face. That sounded okay, but how did she really look? "Am I that flat-chested?" she asked, because she couldn't come out and say "Am I pretty?" That was just too egotistical.

"You're only a little on the small side," Julie said. She gave Toni a reassuring pat on the back. "You'll get there, you're just slow developing."

Toni peered into the music room. Maybe she did it to torture herself. Chorale practice was just starting. Toni should have been in the music room, right in the front row with the other sopranos, or maybe even in the soloist's special place, standing next to the piano. But for the second year in a row she'd chickened out on the auditions. Kay Gibbon stood up, her hands clutched in front of her, her mouth open in a perfect little red O. "How will I know, how will I know . . ." she sang, looking at Mrs. Sokolow, who was accompanying her on the piano, "How will I know . . . if he loves me?"

"Ask him and stop moaning about it," Julie breathed behind Toni, taking her arm. "Come on, I don't want to be late for rehearsal." They went on down the hall to the auditorium.

Ms. Shindy was sitting on the edge of the stage, talking to some of the Drama Society kids. She looked like one of the senior girls in her skinny pants and unlaced high-tops. Toni sat down in back, and Julie went up front. She had a part in the play they were giving just before finals.

During the second act L.R. Faberman came in and sat down across the aisle from Toni. "Holy cow!" she whispered to herself. She riveted her eyes on the stage, sending thoughts to Julie. *L.R. is here . . . L.R. is here . . . L.R. is here. . . .*

The scene ended and Ms. Shindy went up on the stage. "I want to check my voice projection. Are you people able to hear me in back of the auditiorium?" She leaned out. "Who's back there, anyway?"

"It's Toni Chessmore," Julie said.

Everyone in that auditorium turned and looked toward the back. L.R. also turned and looked at Toni.

"Can you hear me back there, Toni Chessmore?"

"Yes," Toni mumbled.

"What?" Ms. Shindy put her hand behind her ear.

"I can hear you."

"You can hear me?"

They could probably hear her in China, Toni thought.

L.R. suddenly stood up. "Yes, we can hear you." He left after that. Why had he come? Why had he left? Toni had no answers, no theories. That was the way the boy was, mysterious.

On the way home she asked Julie if she'd noticed L.R. back there. "Of course," Julie said. "I think he came in to see me. He was there one day last week, too. . . . I think he's rich, Toni. The dark glasses are the giveaway. He wears them every moment of every day. Doesn't that seem superior to you, beautifully arrogant? Exactly the way somebody rich would act?"

Toni mused over this. She had never known anyone rich. Were they really that way, superior, arrogant? Was L.R.? "Are you criticizing him? I thought you were in love with him."

"My child, one thing has nothing to do with another.

It's spicy to criticize. It's *interesting.*" Julie linked her arm with Toni's and pulled her close. "That's why I like being in love! It's interesting, and it gives me something to think about besides my rude parents."

Rude? That was mild compared to some of the things Julie said about her parents. After their last fight Julie had come running over to Toni's house. "I hate them!" she screamed. "I'll never forgive them. I hate their guts. I'd like to rip off their heads. And don't say anything. You don't know what it's like, Toni. Your parents are wonderful, they love each other, they love and adore you."

Toni didn't say anything. How could she, without sounding smug? What Julie had said about her parents was true. They *were* wonderful. It was part of her Toni Luck. It was part of *her.*

• CHAPTER •
THREE

"Toni!" In her room, Toni heard Julie calling her. She went to the window. Julie was below, on the lawn. "Toni, I'm coming up." A minute later she burst into Toni's room. "My stupid parents are at it again. My father quit his job. He just got it two months ago!"

"Oh, Julie—" Toni began, reaching out to her friend.

Julie jerked away. "Don't say it! Don't say you're sorry. And don't tell me you understand, because you don't." She threw herself down on the bed. "Your father works, he always has the same job, your mother doesn't have to grovel for money. Your parents get along, your whole life isn't ruined by them."

"My parents fight sometimes," Toni said.

Julie blew disbelievingly between her lips. "You call that fighting? They don't fight, they *bicker*. That's different, take it from me, that's a huge difference."

Toni sat down next to Julie and tried to think of something to say to her, something positive but not goody-goody. She stroked the glass cat on her bedside table. Her father had bought it for her on her tenth birthday at the factory in Corning. They had driven down there together to pick it out. It was hand-blown, all curves and shining smoothness, the tiny glass whiskers so fine that they seemed to tremble as if in a breeze.

"You know, Julie, when your father's not working, he does things around your house. Remember when he painted your desk? And he does things for other people. Remember when he went all the way to Utica to pick up a part for my mother's car?"

"He's all heart." Julie pushed the pillow behind her head. "You know what he kept saying to my mother? *Don't worry*. 'Don't worry, Jerrine, I'll get another job. This one wasn't suited to my temperament. Don't worry about the bills, Jerrine. Don't worry, I know what I'm doing.' Don't worry, don't worry! Do you know how many times he said it? I counted. When I got to twenty, I left."

"Are you sleeping over?" Toni asked.

"Yes, I'm sleeping over! I'm sick of hearing them. I don't see how Heather can stand all that disgusting noise."

"Heather is leather," Toni said.

Julie gave her a quick smile. "Toni, I'm never going to make it to eighteen living there."

"Yes you are."

"I have to get away."

"You can't, Jul. You have to finish school." This wasn't the first time they'd had this conversation.

"I don't need school to be an actress."

"Julie, you're going to go to a college where they have a really great drama department, and you're going to learn all kinds of stuff, and then you're going to be discovered."

Julie made a terrible face and started breathing hard. "What if I go crazy first?"

"You won't, Julie."

"How do you know?" Now her eyes were filling. Her lips trembled.

"I won't let you go crazy."

"Promise?"

Toni put her arm around Julie. "I promise."

"Sacred promise?"

"Sacred promise," Toni said.

Julie closed her eyes briefly. "Okay," she said after a moment. "Okay."

Every year on Toni's birthday, the plum tree below her bedroom window was in blossom. Her father had planted it on her first birthday, and every morning of her life it was the first thing she saw, bare black branches in winter, white flowers in spring, and tiny red plums in summer.

Her father used to sing to her in her crib, a song of his own making. "Babyface, my dear little babyface, you are the sweetest little neatest little babyface. . . ." Maybe, Toni thought, that was how she'd gotten her love of music—her father's face over her crib like a giant daddy balloon, his deep voice singing just to her. Her parents thought it was impossible that she remembered that, but she did.

Sometimes, if he was moved to do it, her father would sing that song on her birthday. Toni hoped he didn't do it this year. Julie and she were having a joint birthday party with their families. They almost always did, and almost always, for one reason or another, somebody wouldn't show up. Two years before, Heather had been down with a cold. Another year, Toni's mother had gone to New York City to be with Toni's sister, Martine, when she was having an operation.

This year it was Toni's father. She didn't have to worry about his singing to her in front of everyone. He was on duty at the firehouse and wasn't able to trade time. For a while it looked like Julie's father wasn't going to make it to the party, either. He'd taken off on his motorcycle on a jaunt to Atlantic City a few days earlier, to see a wrestling match and maybe do a little gambling. But at the last moment—they were already at the table in Julie's house—he showed up with his helmet in one hand and a bunch of yellow flowers in the other.

"Bought you these posies with my last ten dollars," he said to Julie's mother.

Mrs. Jensen stared at her husband. He was a tall, thin man who liked to wear scarves tossed around his neck. Mrs. Jensen was pretty but tired-looking. She had the same sort of flashing, bulgy blue eyes and blond hair as Julie and Heather. "Flowers?" she said.

"Flowers," he said, bending almost from the waist toward her. He was smiling and staring back at her, and Toni wondered if they were going to explode into one of their fights right in front of everyone. Her stomach tensed at the possibility.

Then Mrs. Jensen took the flowers and stuffed them in a jar. "Well, thank you, Steven," she said.

"You're welcome, my darling."

Under the table, Toni toed Julie, who gave her a relieved look, then got up to get a plate for her father.

After the food but before the cake, Toni's mother and Mrs. Jensen brought in the girls' presents. Julie and Toni went from one box to the next, tearing paper and throwing ribbons into the air. "These girls don't know how fortunate they are," Julie's mother said. She was smoothing out the ribbons to use again.

"I never had a birthday party," Julie whispered from the corner of her mouth to Toni.

"I never had a birthday party," Mrs. Jensen said. "You know, Violet," she said to Toni's mother, "my folks were hired-out farm workers."

Every year Mrs. Jensen said the same thing on their birthday. "I had two rich cousins I hated because I had to wear their old skirts and blouses."

"Even their underwear," Julie whispered.

"Even their underwear," Mrs. Jensen said.

"Oh, that would never do for my Toni," her mother said. And then *she* started telling the same story she told every year—how when Toni was little, she loved the story of the fairy godmothers crowding around the princess's cradle, blessing her with wonderful wishes like beauty, wisdom, and happiness.

"Here was this little mite, and she always cried when I came to the part where the jealous fairy godmother wishes the princess will fall into an everlasting sleep," Toni's mother said. "She would pipe up in her little voice, 'I don't want the princess to sleep forever. I want her to be happy forever.' "

Heather rolled her eyes. "Oh, how adorable."

"Happy forever," Mrs. Jensen echoed. She looked at Mr. Jensen, who was tipped back in his chair, yawning. "Isn't that something, how we think things like that are possible when we're kids?"

"And a good thing we think so," Toni's mother said. "Otherwise we might never get out of bed."

Mrs. Jensen gave an abrupt laugh. "How true!" She got up and brought in the cake. It was frosted in white and covered with candles. Toni counted. Thirty candles. Fourteen for each of them, plus one each to grow on.

"Speech! Speech!" Heather said. "Toni, make a speech." Heather gleamed. She knew she was putting Toni on the spot.

Julie rescued her. "Shut up, Heather. We have to wish on the candles."

Julie and Toni held hands and bent over the cake together. Toni closed her eyes. What could she wish for? She didn't want to change anything in her life. It was perfect. Well, nearly. She could wish for her mother not to tell that same story on her birthday again next year, but that was so trivial. Finally she wished for nothing in her life to change.

When she told Julie later, Julie said, "That wasn't my wish, kiddo! I wished for tons of changes."

• CHAPTER •
FOUR

"Julie's eating supper with us, Mom," Toni said. "She's going to sleep over, too." She kissed her mother, who had just come home from work. "I smell licorice."

Her mother felt around in the pockets of her jacket and came up with a string of red licorice. "I saved it for you. . . . What's with Julie?"

Toni got plates from the cupboard. "Her parents."

"Again?" Her mother moved quickly around the kitchen. She took an aerobics class once a week and ran four miles every other morning. "I'm fifty, I can't let myself slow down," she would say. "Because once you start slowing down, you start running down."

"How did you like that caraway cheese I put in your lunch?" She was constantly trying to fatten Toni up. At the supper table, though, when Toni's father sliced a chunk of the same cheese, her mother's reaction was different. "Hal—calories and cholesterol."

Her father cut a second slice. "Babyface, tell the skinny woman that the fireman eats whatever he wants because he's in shape."

"Sweetie," her mother said, "tell the overweight one that he hasn't been in any kind of shape for more years than he wants to count."

Babyface, tell her . . . Babyface, tell him . . . For as long as Toni could remember, her parents had played this game. When she could barely walk, they had sent her with messages to deliver in her baby voice from one to the other. She would be rewarded with a hug, a kiss, laughter.

Toni passed the rolls to Julie. "You people are very cute, but cut it out now." Her father saluted. They both liked it when she bossed them around. "Dad," she said, "Mom has a point, though. We were hearing in health class about obesity—"

"Hey, hey, hey. You calling me names?" He sat there, a massive man with a round smiling red face. Every room was always too hot for him. "You think I'm fat? You getting together with your mother on this?"

"Daddy, you could lose a little bit of weight. And I worry about you smoking. You know what Julie calls you? A smoking maniac."

"Thank you very much, Toni," Julie said.

The phone rang in the kitchen, and Toni went to answer it. It was her sister. "Martine here," she said. "Is this Toni?"

Who did she think it was? "Hi, Martine."

"Is Mom there, then? May I speak to her, please?"

Whenever her sister called, it was always, "Hello, is this Toni? Is Mom there?" Once in a while she'd ask to talk to their father. But never, Toni thought, never did her sister take an extra breath to talk to her. Would it hurt her to say "Toni, what's doing with you? How's your life? What're your thoughts on the world?" But maybe she thought Toni had no thoughts, or none that she would be interested in, anyway.

When her mother came back to the table after getting off the phone, her face was flushed. "Well, guess what? Martine's engaged to that nice man she told us about. Alex Grant, the one who sells real estate."

Toni gave Julie a look and held up three fingers, meaning this was the third time her sister had been engaged. Each time before, her mother had been just as happy. And each time when Martine broke the engagement, Toni's mother had said it was for the best.

Later Toni and Julie went into the family room with their homework. Julie shoved a cassette into the VCR. She was an old-movie freak. "*North by Northwest* is a classic, Toni. Cary Grant is adorable. I love that dimple."

"As adorable as L.R. Faberman?"

Julie shoved her. "It's different. Cary is old and adorable. L.R. is young and adorable."

"I think you should talk to him."

"I will when the time is right," Julie said.

"When is that going to be?"

"I don't know. Maybe soon."

"Are you worried about talking to him?" *She* would be if she were in love with someone.

"No, I always have things to talk about. You know what I'm really worried about? What if he's dull? Then I won't have anybody to be in love with." Julie leaned forward. "Wait, don't talk, this is one of my favorite parts."

Toni found the movie not terribly interesting. The heroine, an actress named Eva Marie Saint, had hair like gold cement. Ditto her face, not a quiver of emotion. Maybe Toni's sister and Eva were the same type. She picked up the framed picture of Martine that was on the end table, her high-school graduation picture.

Toni had been only two years old and didn't remember that time, but then she didn't remember very much about Martine, who had been fifteen years old when Toni was born. Two years later Martine had gone to college. Since then, except for brief visits sometimes, over the holidays, she rarely came home. They were like strangers, Toni thought. If she wrote her a letter, she'd have to begin not with *Dear Sister*, but *Dear Stranger*.

Dear Stranger,

I find it amazing we came from the same parents. We are not at all alike. You're tall, beautiful, graceful, you've got a great business head. You got some very fine gifts from the fairy godmothers at your cradle! Do you know what I'm saying? Do you like reading? Did you read fairy tales when you were a kid? Did Mom read to you? Did Dad sing to you?

I have an idea that sisters should be special to each other. I can see from watching Heather and Julie in action that I'm probably right off the track, being sentimental. I don't think you're sentimental, so probably it won't bother you at all when I say that sometimes I forget I even have a sister. Well, I know you won't write back, because I won't send this letter. And I won't send it because I know you wouldn't write me back, even if I did send it! (Remember the year I wrote you three times? No? I didn't think so. You never answered.) Well, good-bye for now, until the next time I feel like writing you a letter I won't send.

Toni

P.S. My music teacher in fifth grade wrote in my autograph book, "Never B Flat, Always B Sharp, Always B True to Yourself." I tried to take that to heart. I thought it meant I should always be honest. Maybe that's one thing we *do* have in common. Since you have no interest in me, it's probably very honest of you not to pretend that you do.

"You've got to watch this part." Julie shook Toni's arm. "This is my favorite scene. Cary Grant is *so* cool." She spoke his line with him, in a clipped English accent. " 'I haven't let anybody take off my clothes since I was a little boy.' "

" 'But you're a big boy now,' " Eva Marie Saint and Julie drawled together.

A few minutes later Toni's father came in. Julie flashed a smile. "Mr. Chessmore, are you going to watch the movie with us? You'll probably enjoy it."

"She lies, Dad," Toni said. "It's boring."

Her father pulled up a chair. "Is it hot in here?"

"Not especially, Dad."

He wiped his forehead with a red bandanna. "Are you girls comfortable?"

"I'll open a window for you," Toni said.

"Oh, don't bother, Babyface," he said. But she got up, anyway, and opened both windows.

• CHAPTER •
FIVE

Kelly Lutz sat down at the lunch table next to Toni and opened a carton of chocolate milk. "Just the color my hair used to be," she remarked. Kelly had dyed her hair again. It looked as if she had a purple veil spread over it. "Aren't you eating your lunch?" she said to Julie.

"I don't happen to be hungry."

"Looks like a good lunch. Did your mother make it?"

"Yes."

"Are you on a diet?"

Julie pushed aside her sandwich. "What are you, Lutz, the lunchroom spy? For your information, I never diet."

"Good. You should hear my mother on the subject. No! *Nada!* I can't even drink a diet soda in front of her. If I don't clean up my plate, she has a fit. She says I have a gorgeous figure just the way I am." Kelly rolled her eyes. "Can I help it if my mother thinks I hung the moon?"

"Fascinating." Julie clipped off the word. Her cheeks were burning. She got up and left the cafeteria.

"What's her problem?" Kelly said.

Just what Toni had been wondering. She picked up Julie's

purse. She'd forgotten it in her rush to get away. "See you," she said to Kelly.

Toni didn't see Julie anywhere in the halls. She went outside. Julie was across the street, sitting on the stoop of the corner store. Toni crossed and sat down next to her. "Are you all right?" She handed Julie her purse. Julie took out a cigarette and tapped it on the back of her hand.

"Jul, what is it?" Toni put her hand on her friend's arm. "Is it your parents?"

"Of course it's my parents. Is it ever anything else?" She jerked the cigarette in and out of her mouth. "I'm not going to be here this summer, Toni. I'll be in San Francisco."

"San Francisco?" Toni said, as if she'd never heard of it.

"Mom, Heather, and I are going away as soon as school is over," Julie said flatly. "My parents are splitting. My father's taking off for Alaska and we're going out West."

"They're getting a divorce?" Toni said disbelievingly.

Julie crushed her cigarette underfoot. "I don't know. All I know is that my father says he has to see Alaska before he dies. And my mother says she's not hanging around Ridgewood all summer with everything dumped on her, that she has to have something for herself, too."

"Oh, Julie," Toni said. She couldn't think of a single comforting thing to say to Julie, or to herself. She and Julie had never spent even one summer apart.

"I wish I could do something to Julie's parents," Toni said to her mother. What she had in mind was homicide, but what she said was "I'd like to shake them till their teeth rattle!"

Her mother raised her eyebrows. She was stretched out

in a bubble bath. "I just wonder what in the world Steven is going to do in Alaska."

"Maybe he'll teach the polar bears to drive motorcycles."

"Toni!" Her mother laughed.

Toni picked up the loofah and scrubbed her mother's back. "Julie's parents never think of anyone but themselves. Heather's all excited about San Francisco, so it's okay for her, but Julie's just sick about it, and so am I."

"I know it's going to be hard for you without her, but you'll survive, sweetie."

"I don't want to survive. I want Julie to be here." Toni sat on the edge of the tub, brooding. "Mom, why can't Julie stay with us? Why does she have to go if she doesn't want to?" Toni sat up. Why hadn't she thought of this right away?

"Live *here*? I don't think that's a good idea, sweetie."

"Why not? Julie and I would be together all the time," Toni argued. "You wouldn't even know she was here. She wouldn't be any extra work."

Her mother put a soapy hand on Toni's arm. "First of all, I doubt that Jerrine would agree to leave Julie behind. But even if she did, having the responsibility for another person for that long a time is something I'd have to think about very hard. What if something happened to her?"

"What could happen? Nothing will happen. I promise you! Mom, please! Please, Mom, I'll get down on my hands and knees," Toni said, reverting to a childhood phrase that used to make her parents laugh and almost always got her whatever she wanted, whether it was extra TV or a candy bar.

Her mother got out of the tub and wrapped herself in a

towel. "Anyway, the whole thing might not even happen. It could be a tempest in a teapot." She held up her hand, pushing down fingers, one at a time. "Steven might not go to Alaska. Jerrine might decide it's too much trouble to close up the house. Or too much trouble to take herself all the way to San Francisco. Or they might make up. You never know. Circumstances change. . . ."

Her mother rubbed cream into her legs. "Are you listening, sweetie? I know what I'm talking about. I know from experience that people say things, but they don't necessarily carry them out. It's human nature."

Toni nodded, but she didn't think her mother really understood how she felt about Julie going away. And if her mother didn't understand, then nobody could. Take something like camping in the backyard. Every summer when the heat got bad, she and Julie would pitch her pop-up tent and camp out with books and food and flashlights. It was something they looked forward to all year. It was special, something that was theirs and theirs alone. They'd even promised themselves that after they were grown and married and had children of their own, they would still get together and camp in the summer.

Toni had never thought much about time before. If she had thought about it at all, she probably would have said it was like a friend who brought her good things. She had never especially wanted to hurry time up, or slow it down. But that was before Julie told her about San Francisco. Now Toni wanted to pounce on time, take it by the neck, grab it around the ankle, hold it. Hold it back! Slow it down!

• CHAPTER •
SIX

The day Julie left, Toni went to the airport with her. They had said good-bye in private (they had stayed up till nearly morning, talking) and agreed that they wouldn't be emotional in front of Julie's mother and sister. Maybe they were too quiet. "Somone make a joke," Heather ordered. She was sitting up front with the driver.

"Shut up, Heather," Julie said automatically. She leaned her head against the window.

"I want a joke!" Heather said. "Toni! Give me a joke."

"What song was the woman who came back from India singing?" Toni obliged. Her father had read the joke out loud from the morning paper. He was a sucker for corny jokes.

"I saw that. 'Whose Sari now,' " Heather said in a bored voice.

In the airport, Toni took a picture of Julie. Mrs. Jensen was sitting to one side, checking things in her purse. "Take my picture," Heather said, posing with one hand to her hair.

"Put your arm around Julie. I'll take you two together."

"What's the matter, you don't like my face alone?" Heather got her hands around Julie's neck in a choke hold. "How's this for a pose?"

"Heather, damn it!" Julie pushed her sister away.

"Girls, please." Mrs. Jensen rubbed her forehead. "I have enough to think about." She stood up. "Let's go through security now. Good-bye, Toni." She kissed her on the cheek. "Tell your mother I'll be in touch. She knows where to get me if there're any problems."

Toni nodded. Her mother was going to look out for the Jensens' house. Not that there was much to do. Toni had said she'd keep the grass cut.

"We'll see you all in the fall," Mrs. Jensen said. She put her shoulder bag on the moving belt and walked through the security arch. Heather followed her. Then Julie put her purse down in front of the little curtain. Her eyes were glistening. Toni lunged forward and hugged her.

"Come on, Julie," her mother called from the other side. "You're holding up people." Julie walked through the arch, then went slowly down the corridor after her mother and out of sight.

Outside, Toni waited for the bus back to the city. She heard the roar of a jet taking off and shaded her eyes to watch it for a moment, even though she knew it was too soon to be Julie's plane.

• CHAPTER •
SEVEN

June 26

Dearest Julie,

The two days since you left have been long and horrible. I miss you so much. I hate looking across at your house with the shades all pulled down. I even miss Heather (I think). Mom just went off to work. Dad's on for forty-eight hours at the station. Just Paws and me rattling around in the house. Yesterday I weeded the flower bed. Today I'll bake peanut-butter cookies, a special request from my father. I had to promise to use his recipe. He said he spent many long hours taste-testing to get it right!

Send me a letter soon!

Love always,
Toni

June 29

Dear Toni,

The last time we visited my Aunt Wendy I was eight years old. I'd forgotten how small her house is, just three little rooms tucked away at the end of an alley behind two huge Victorian-type houses. To get to Wendy's house from the street you unlatch a gate, duck under the arch, and walk down the alley between the two big houses.

Mom is sharing the bedroom with Wendy. I get to sleep on the pullout couch in the living room with Heather. The girl kicks like a mule half the night, grabs all the covers, and never shuts up, not even when she's sleeping. I miss you, too. I think about home and you, and even Paws, the Slimeball Killer Kat. (I won't go so far as to say I miss *him.*)

Write soon.

Love you much,
Julie

July 5

Dear Julie,

Here's what I do every day. Read, read, read. Take a million showers to keep cool. Watch old reruns of *The Honeymooners* and *Leave It to Beaver.* Today I walked over to the mall just so I could then walk back home again with Mom. Isn't that exciting?

On the way over I found a five-dollar bill. Toni Luck! When I got to the drugstore, I saw a sign in the window for part-time help. I asked Mom to hire me. She said she couldn't hire a relative, it wouldn't be fair. But it gave me the idea that I should get a job. If you were here, we'd put an ad in the paper together: "Willing teens want to help with housework, baby care, dog-sitting, and errands." We'd share the work, split the pay, have plenty of fun, and be rich at the end of the summer!

Love you high, wide, and forever,
Toni

P.S. My father's trying to cheer me up with jokes. Today's joke is "Did you hear about the woman arrested on charges of illegal possession of a fireman?"

July 13

Dear Toni,

Your letter took a week to get here. I think they sent it by Pony Express. See, I can make a joke, too. My mother accuses me of not having a sense of humor anymore. She might be right. Every morning I wake up and think about home and start feeling upset and horrible and end up fighting with someone.

Mom says I should try to be more positive. I say, "It's easy for you to say. You *want* to be here!" Mom says, "Julie, you're right, and I'm sorry, but that's the way it is now. Isn't there *anything* good for you in this situation?" I say, "No! Nothing!" I can tell I make her feel awful. Do you think I'm a total bitch?

Love, Julie

P.S. Wendy says it's harder to find a kid job here than a rat's tail in chicken soup. Whatever that means. Wendy has some weird expressions.

July 16

Dear Julie,

Today my father called from the station and asked me to bring him a fresh T-shirt. I biked over. Dad and a bunch of other men were outside washing one of the trucks. Buckets of suds, huge streams of water. It's like seeing an elephant getting a shower. I gave my father his shirt and I was ready to leave, but my father said, "Wait a second, Babyface. Guys, do you all know my beautiful little girl?"

And then, as if what Dad had said was a secret code or something, they all started teasing me. Eddy Mason (I think you know him, he's bald with the freckles on his head, my father's fishing buddy) started it off. "Do we know your little girl, Hal? Do we *know* her? Is this the *famous* Toni Chessmore? The one they write newspaper articles about?" Then they all jumped in. "What's it like to be a celebrity? When are you going on the Johnny Carson show? How old are you now? Do you have to keep the guys away with a baseball bat? Do you want to be a lady fire fighter?" (They thought that one was *really* hilarious.)

Riding home, I thought of all the things I could have said. "What's so funny about a woman being a fire fighter?" Or "If I go on the Johnny Carson show, you'll be the first to know!" Wouldn't it be cool if you knew beforehand what people were going to say, so you could get prepared with smart answers?

Love you forever and always,

Toni

July 22

Dear Toni,

Today I'm lying around reading old magazines and watching TV, because the weather is too nasty for a human being used to normal summers. It's cold, the wind is blowing, the fog is in. It's like being in the middle of a horror movie. Can you imagine having to wear two sweaters to keep from freezing to death in the middle of the summer?

Let's see, what else exciting can I tell you? Oh, yes, yesterday Wendy showed me some tall green weedy stuff in an empty lot down the street. "Do you know what that is, Julie?" "No, Aunt Wendy." "Dill, Julie." "Dill, Aunt Wendy? The little seedy stuff that comes in jars and my mother likes on mustard-and-cheese sandwiches?" "Yes, Julie." Well, well, learn something new every day.

The big news here is that Mom has decided she has to make some money and so she's going to sell cosmetics again. She bought a car. She says even though she has to make car payments, she'll make more money in the long run. I sure hope so, I hate being poor. Well, that's it for now.

Lots of love,

Julie

July 31

Dear Julie,

Hooray! The end of the month! One down, one to go!

Well, guess what? I have a job! How I got it is pure Toni Luck. Yesterday I saw little Arnold Frankowitz from down the street pulling a wagon. I said, "I like your haircut, Arnie." He put his hands on his hips and said, "No Arnie stuff. I'm Arnold." I asked him how old he was. He held up three fingers. "Nice wagon," I said. And he said, "I have to clean this vagon, it's dirty."

Then, Julie, his mom leaned over the porch and said, "Toni, how would you like a job? All you'd have to do is take Arnold to the park and play with him for a couple hours every morning." And she told me some rules, like Arnold can't have anything with sugar. She pointed to her teeth, which are kind of small and gray, and said she didn't want him to have teeth like hers. I start tomorrow.

Love,
Toni

• CHAPTER • EIGHT

August 1

Dear Toni,

Today for some reason I feel happier. It's August 1, which means this lousy summer is going to end in thirty more days. I told my mother, "I'm counting down." She said, "Why not count the good things about being here?" I said, "Like what?"

We were sitting at the table in the kitchen. My aunt said, "Julie, I don't know anyone in the world who can resist the beauty of San Francisco. It's a city of hills and water."

More "Yeah, yeah" from Julie. But not so loud. Because that is one of the things I do like about being here. If you get up high enough, you can look down over the city and out into the bay and the ocean. And that is neat.

Love you,
Julie

August 5

Dear Toni,

I just wrote a couple days ago, but I feel inspired to write again. So you've got a job, and it sounds perfect. Nothing for me yet. Heather has been working at a sandwich shop, washing dishes. She loaned me ten dollars. Then she gave (not loaned) Mom twenty. Mom went crazy. "Oh, Heather, you're such a wonderful daughter!"

I felt about as high as a worm's belly. I wouldn't mind doing something great and having Mom fall all over me. Maybe someday she'll see me in a movie or up on the stage and say, "That's *my* daughter."

Love,
Julie

August 8

Dear Julie,

Taking care of Arnold isn't quite the piece of cake I expected. This kid could wear us *both* out. He is perpetual motion. In the park I follow him from sandbox to swings to slides to sandbox to swings to—well, you get the idea. He is also perpetual *mouth*. "Toni, do you have a broom in your house like I do in my house? Toni, do you have a stove in your house like I do in my house? Toni, do you have a bed in your house like I do in my house?"

I try saying "Arnold, I have *everything* in my house." That doesn't stop him for a second. "Toni, do you have a sofa in your house? Do you have a potty in your house? Do you have a daddy in your house? Do you have a jar in your house?" He can go on like this for hours.

And then there's the soda crisis. When he gets thirsty, his mom says he has to drink water. This is not Arnold's favorite drink. What does he vant? "I vant soda!" he yells. He whirls around. His face turns red. He's having a tantrum! He's making me crazy!

Today I had an inspiration. He was whirling and yelling, and I told him he was really funny because he didn't know water was *delicious.* I patted my stomach. I said, "I'm going to get some of that delicious water for myself, right now!" Arnold trotted after me. "I vant a drink of vater!" I said, "Oh, no, you don't like it." He said, "Yes, I vant vater!" I said, "Well, maybe . . ."

Jul, he drank that water like it was the world's greatest drink. I'm proud of myself. I didn't let a three-year-old squirt (pardon the pun) get the best of me.

Love,
Toni

August 9

Dear Julie,

This morning I walked over to the drugstore to see Mom. Guess who I saw working there? L.R. Faberman! Same black T-shirt, same dark glasses, same adorable face. I forgot all about saying hello to Mom. Instead I bought a few things and stood in his checkout line. I thought, *What am I doing?* My stomach felt as if a bunch of ice cubes were down there doing a dance.

I put my stuff down and took out money. L.R. rang it up and gave me change. I said, "You're L.R. Faberman." He said, "Yes. How do you know that?" I could have said, "You sat right across from me in the auditorium, dummy!" (Another one of my clever replies I think of too late.) What I said was, "We both go to Emerson." And *then* I said, "You, me, and *Julie Jensen.*" I don't know where I got the nerve! What do you think of that, Julie?

Love, hugs, and kisses,
Toni

August 12

Dear Toni,

To be truthful, L.R. seems like someone I knew a million years ago. Or should I say someone I *didn't* know? I can't even think what he looks like. Toni, this is what's on my mind—Mom is talking about staying on for another month. I can't understand her. I don't know how her mind works. All she'll say is she's not prepared to go home as long as my father is still in Alaska. What's one thing got to do with the other?

Love,
Julie

August 12

Dear Julie,

My father's had a heart attack. I'm scared. I don't want him to die. Pray for him.

Love,
Toni

• CHAPTER •
NINE

The intensive care unit was noisy and bright with lights. Machines hummed, hissed, and burped; nurses and doctors talked in loud, fast voices. "You can have ten minutes," the duty nurse told Toni and her mother. They walked past rows of beds with white-sheeted forms hooked into all kinds of machines and monitors. Her mother stopped at a bed at the bottom of the left-hand row.

Toni slowly approached the bed. Was that really her father? She had never seen him lie so still. He was not a still man. He was always busy with something around the house. Even when he took a nap on the couch, he was in motion, twitching, mumbling, turning from side to side. But now he lay without movement, covered by a white sheet.

"Daddy." She kissed his cheek. His eyes opened and he raised a hand slowly, then let it drop.

Her mother stood on the other side of the bed. His head turned slowly toward her. "Going to say 'I told you so'?" he whispered.

"Shhh," her mother said.

So of course he began talking. It was painful to hear him speak. "I . . . was . . . asleep . . . at the station," he began. Each word came out separately, with little puffs of breath between them. "Woke up around five with a bad . . . feeling in my chest. I ate . . . fried onion rings last night."

"Fried onion rings," her mother said on a sigh. "Hal. Kid food."

"I . . . took antacid, got dressed. . . . Still in pain, thought I was going to pass out. . . ."

Toni leaned closer and took her father's hand.

"Eddy . . . called the ambulance." His eyes closed.

"Where is he?" a booming voice called just then. "Where is that old faker?" It was Eddy Mason himself, holding his hat. His bald, freckled head shone under the lights. He grabbed Toni's father's feet through the white sheet. "Hal, what the hell is this, lying around resting in the middle of the day?"

Her father's eyes opened. "They told me . . . I'm going to have to . . . take it easy for a while."

"Don't believe it, Mrs. Chessmore," Eddy said. "This guy's a working fool. He's going to be back at the station answering four alarms by the end of the week." He winked at Toni.

• CHAPTER •
TEN

August 14

Dear Julie,

At home, the phone doesn't stop ringing for a moment. My sister flew in this morning to see Dad. Mom and I were at the hospital when she got there. Martine said, "Well, Dad, I'm sorry it had to come to this, but sometimes these things can be blessings in disguise." I wanted to kick her, Julie! Imagine telling him almost dying and being in horrible pain was a blessing!

She didn't stop, either. She said, "I know Mom has wanted you to quit smoking for years, and lose weight, too." And then she told him he actually looked very well. "Better then the last time I saw you," she said, as if the heart attack had been good for him! Sometimes I think my sister dropped down to earth from another galaxy.

Did you ever notice the way hospitals smell, Julie? As soon as I walk in, I notice it. I hate the smell. I probably hate hospitals. I want my father to get better and get out of there and come home! Julie, write me soon.

Love you,
Toni

August 15

Dear Julie,

Did you get my letter about my father? Mom says he's improving every day, but I don't know what to think. He's so changed. You know how he is, always doing something. Well, now he doesn't do anything but lie in bed. The worst part is that he doesn't even complain about it. I know he has to rest his heart, but it scares me. Write, please.

Love,
Toni

August 17

Dear Toni,

I only got your letter today. It took almost a week to get out here. I'm really sorry about your father. I hope he's much better already! Well, if heart attacks happened to kids, *I'd* be a major candidate. Yeah, I'm still smoking, plus I've gained weight, which I *hate* (wish I could give it you), but sometimes there's nothing to do here but eat.

My mother was crying last night. My aunt Wendy kept giving me significant looks and jerking her head toward Mom, meaning she wanted me to say something to make Mom feel better. I know I should have, but I didn't. All I could think was that Mom was the one who brought us out here. It wasn't my idea, or Heather's.

Love, Julie

P.S. Give my love to your father. Give him a hug for me.
P.P.S. I hope you don't think I'm totally selfish, just talking about myself.

August 17

Dear Julie,

My father is out of the ICU. They moved him into a private room a few days ago. But he is still weak and walks down the hospital corridor like an old man, with little shuffly steps. It makes me want to cry.

Julie, can't you talk to your mother about coming back? Tell her you have to be here for school. Don't lose your temper, just talk to her calmly, and I'm sure she'll understand.

Love, Toni

P.S. Do you think about L.R. at all? He's still working in the drugstore. Just thought you'd like to know.

August 20

Dear Toni,

Well, it's official—we're not coming home at the end of the month. Don't scream. I've done enough of that for both of us. Are you ever going to have kids? I'm not. I wouldn't want to screw up someone else's life.

Love,
Julie

August 23

Dear Julie,

Yesterday we went to see the heart specialist, and he told my father the heart attack was a warning. "The next one could be the last one, Mr. Chessmore," he said. He told Dad he had to stop smoking, start exercising, change his diet, and lose weight. My father said he didn't know if he could do all that. He said, "I don't know if I have the willpower."

The doctor wants Dad to go to a place in Ohio called the Hertha Center, where he can be intensively retrained in his habits. Mom asked how long the program was, and Dad asked how much it cost. The doctor answered Mom (ten days), but to Dad he said, "What do you care how much, Mr. Chessmore? Go into debt if you have to. Do you want to live to see your daughter grow up?" I wish he hadn't said that! I felt so sorry for my father. Julie, write me soon.

Love,
Toni

August 24

Dear Julie,

Today I found out that while Mom and Dad go to the Hertha Center I'm to stay with my sister in New

York City. Julie, you know I'd be better off with a total stranger than with Martine! But I'm going on Monday. Mrs. Abish is going to take care of Paws. My next letter to you will be from New York City. Do you think I can survive ten days with my sister, the ice cube? Martine's address is 75 Bank Street, New York City, NY 10011. Write me.

Love you always,
Toni

• CHAPTER •
ELEVEN

The moment she got off the bus, the oily stench from the buses parked one behind another in the dark tunnel made Toni feel queasy. Was it tension? Anxiety? Fear? All of the above? Half of the trip she'd spent wondering if she was on the right bus. The other half, trying to imagine what it would be like spending almost two weeks with a sister she'd never before spent more than two hours with.

She shifted her shoulder bag. The crowd streamed into the building, and Toni followed. "Just wait for me on the second level by the escalator," Martine had said. The second level? Was that where she was now?

She looked around, checking the signs. She seemed to be in the right place. An endless stream of people flowed around her. Where did they all come from? Martine had said firmly that Toni was not to go down into the main terminal. Fine, but what if Martine didn't come? What if she'd forgotten the time? Or the place? Or forgotten Toni altogether? Toni glanced at her watch. She was fast losing the little bit of faith she had in her sister.

Five anxious minutes later she finally saw Martine, coming up the escalator, looking cool in a loose, pale, lettuce-green dress. She always forgot how beautiful her sister was. Martine seemed to float into Toni's eyes. Her hair was in a thick twist on top of her head. Her ears were pierced in many places, and in each one was a little sparkle of color, a tiny jeweled earring.

"Hello, Toni. Sorry I'm late. The traffic . . ." She turned her cheek for Toni's kiss and took the shoulder bag from her. "Is this all you have? How was your trip?"

"I thought you forgot me," Toni blurted.

"I wouldn't do that."

Toni shifted her knapsack and followed her sister through the huge terminal and out into the street. She was unprepared for the noise and heat. "Are you hungry?" Martine asked.

"Not too much," Toni said. Her mother had given her a care package with sandwiches, fruit, and cookies.

"Good, we'll eat at home. We could take the subway down to the Village, but the stations are sweatboxes."

Toni nodded.

"We could cab it, but with the traffic we can probably get there almost as fast walking."

She nodded again.

"Well, which one?"

"Oh. You want me to decide? Uh, walk." How was she supposed to know the best way to go?

Martine veered off the sidewalk where men in hard hats were tearing up the pavement. Toni trotted after her. At the corner Martine crossed, ignoring cars that stopped only inches from them. A man in a T-shirt, his big belly shaking, worked a jackhammer in a cloud of dust.

Toni's head turned one way, then the other, trying to see and hear everything. "Outa the way!" someone yelled, and she leaped aside as two men raced past her carrying a long, rolled-up rug on their shoulders.

"This is the city, Toni," her sister said. "You have to be awake here." Was Toni supposed to thank her for that information?

"Watches, watches," a tall black woman standing behind a little table sang. "The best, the prettiest, the finest watches right here." They passed stores with their wares in bins and racks out on the sidewalk. They passed hills of garbage in black plastic bags, they passed a man sleeping on the sidewalk and other men with their hands out, begging. Ahead of her, Toni heard a man say, "Do I look meaner in this shirt?" And he answered himself, "Yeah, definitely more aggressive." She began to write a letter to Julie in her head.

Dear Julie, the noise in the city is like a slap in the head. It's huge, it's immense, it's like a thing in itself. Trucks pound the streets, horns blow, sirens scream, everyone is talking or yelling.

A woman touched Toni's arm. "Do you have any change for me?" she asked in a soft voice. "I'm hungry." She had a crown of thin gray hair. Toni fumbled in her pocket and gave her all her change. "Oh, thank you," the woman said. "Thank you, dear, thank you!"

"You have to ignore those people," her sister said when Toni caught up with her.

"She was hungry, Martine."

"Thirsty, more likely," Martine said tartly.

Dear Julie, Remember that day in the girls' room when you shouted "Witch with a B!*" after Heather? Well, in my opinion, compared to Martine, Heather is a heavenly angel.*

They stopped for a red light, and Martine balanced on the edge of the curb, glancing down the street. "I'm glad you took a late bus," she said. "It would have been a hassle for me to leave work early."

Well, good, she had done *something* right, anyway. She knew Martine worked in a brokerage firm and that it had something to do with money. "What do you do at work?" she said. And hastily, before her sister could say, "What do I do? I *work,*" she said, "I mean, I know you're a broker."

"Right. Our firm goes all over the world," Martine said. For the first time she became animated. "It's fascinating work. Wednesday I phoned England. Friday I was on the line to Japan."

"How did you talk to them?"

"What do you mean by that?"

"Well . . . Japan. You don't speak Japanese, do you?"

"The Japanese all speak English. But for the most part I'm talking to Americans. Americans live and work in other countries too," she lectured, as if Toni didn't know anything. And to drive home the point she said, "There's a great deal more to the world than little Ridgewood."

Dear Julie, I haven't even been here an hour yet, and already I'm wondering how I'm going to manage ten days!

"How did Dad seem these last few days?" Martine asked. "Mom told me the doctor says he's got to change the way he's living, lose weight, et cetera."

Toni nodded and looked at her watch. Her parents' plane

would have landed in Cleveland hours ago. They were probably all settled in now.

"Well, maybe something good will come out of the heart attack," Martine went on. "Dad had terrible habits. He's very self-destructive. He's needed to lose weight for years, he's always been too fat."

Not that fat, Toni thought furiously.

Before they got to her apartment, Martine stopped to buy groceries. The fruits and vegetables at the Light of Spring Deli Market were outside, displayed like jewels on sloping stands. A man with black hair said to Martine, "You want bananas tonight? Nice yellow color to go with your green dress."

Bananas to go with Martine's dress? Something else to write Julie.

"Beautiful colors, yellow and green," the man said.

Her sister bought the bananas.

• CHAPTER •
TWELVE

"I hope you're not one of those people who thrash around all night," Martine said. "I'm a light sleeper." She cleared the last of their supper dishes off the table.

"I can sleep on the couch," Toni said. It had wooden arms and two pillows against a wooden back.

"The couch is too small to sleep on. We'd have to saw you in half to make you fit." Amusing thought? She smiled.

"Everything is small here," Toni said neutrally. The kitchen was no bigger than a closet. The red rug between the couch and a small matching wooden chair was the size of a spot.

"Not small," Martine corrected her, "*scaled.* The furniture is scaled to the apartment."

Toni nodded. She didn't know how Martine could keep saying the word *apartment* with a straight face. It was one small room, plus the tiny kitchen and, if possible, an even tinier bathroom. The whole place could have fit nicely into their living room at home, with plenty of room to spare.

Martine went into the bathroom. Toni heard the shower. A few minutes later the phone rang. It was Toni's parents, first her father on the phone, then her mother, then her father again, both of them asking questions. "How was the trip? . . . Did Martine meet you all right? . . . Are you all settled in? . . . Did you go out to eat supper? . . . How are you and Martine getting along? . . . So how do you like the big city?" They wanted to know everything.

Toni would have talked a lot longer, but her parents had to go off to another orientation session. Her mother came back on the phone. "Give Martine my love, Toni. I'll call again in a few days. And you have a wonderful time, sweetheart. Good-bye, Toni. I love you."

"I love you, Mom."

After she hung up, Toni got into her pajamas. Her knapsack and bag were on the couch. Maybe Martine would give her a place to put things in the closet, though it didn't look like it had an extra inch of space. It was packed from floor to ceiling with clothes, shoes, boxes, and bags.

Toni sat down on the couch. Not too comfortable. She sat on the chair. A moment later she tried the bed. Hard. It was a double mattress on the floor, or more exactly, a futon on the floor. There was a little goosenecked lamp pinned to the wall. Under it were a few polished stones arranged on a tiny mat around a framed picture of Alex, Martine's fiancé. At the foot of the futon was a little bureau with a tiny TV on top, and next to it was a clock about as big as a pack of matches. It was nine-thirty.

Martine came out of the bathroom, her skin glistening, her hair in wet snakes around her face. "Mom called," Toni said. "She sent you her love."

"Is she okay?" Martine asked. "How's Dad doing?"

Toni nodded. "Good."

"I'm beat," her sister said. "I want to go to sleep now. Lights out. Okay with you?"

What was Toni supposed to say? *No, I want to keep the lights on and keep you awake.* She lay down and discovered she was tired. She'd been up since early that morning.

"Move," Martine said, standing over her. She pointed toward the wall. Toni moved. "More." She moved again. Martine nodded and shut off the light. "If you're going to thrash," she said into the darkness, "thrash that way. Toward the wall."

"I don't thrash," Toni muttered under her breath. She lay still, her back to her sister, listening to Martine's breathing. Images, words, colors, and sounds tumbled through her mind. She was in the bus . . . walking down the street . . . almost asleep, but then her knees started to ache. She didn't dare move, for fear of disturbing Martine. Her eyes blinked open. Light came in from the street. She heard someone cough. Then, over her head, a thump, a yell, and her heart skittered. She thought she'd never sleep.

She woke up to the hum of the air conditioner and the sun burning through the windows. Martine was gone. Toni dressed, folded sheets, threw the cover over the bed, and made herself something to eat. She washed the dishes. "Now what?" she said out loud. She pushed aside her clothes on the couch and sat down, suddenly, horribly, surprised by the thought of where she was.

Out the window, she watched a double line of yellow taxis, all going the same way and all blowing their horns furiously. In Ridgewood, if they saw a taxi once a year, it was an event. Someone had left a gray couch out on the sidewalk. A man came around the corner. He was wearing dark pants, a heavy jacket, a hat pulled over his face. What was the matter with him? Why was he dressed like that in the middle of the summer?

All at once, Toni was frantic to smell fresh air. There were two windows, both locked, one barred on the outside. She tugged at the unbarred window, but she couldn't get it open. Her eyes blurred. She leaned her forehead against the glass. "I don't want to be here!" she whispered. "I don't want to be in here!" But where could she go? Out? What would she do out alone on the streets of New York? She didn't know anyone. She didn't know her way around. She hated this filthy, noisy, ugly city! She should have stayed home. She'd wanted to, but her mother had said no, absolutely not.

"I wouldn't have a moment's peace," her mother had said. "At least, with you at Martine's, I'll know you're being looked after." What a joke! Martine wouldn't be back until the end of the day. Toni was going to be alone all day, every day. What had her mother been afraid of in their own home? Nothing would have happened to her there. Here was where it was dangerous—this city, the streets, the people! They just weren't like they were in Ridgewood. People here were bizarre.

As if to prove her point, at that moment Toni saw a strange sight out the window. A woman wearing baggy shorts and a colored T-shirt sat down on the couch, took a can of soda out of a paper bag, and sat there, drinking it and reading a newspaper, as if she were in her own living room. She sat there for at least ten minutes. Before she left, she carefully plumped up all the pillows.

August 28

Dear Julie,

Writing this on my first day in Newyorkcity. How I wish it was my last. I've been looking out the window of Martine's apartment for hours. Watching what goes on in the street is sort of like living TV, only you never get the end of the story. For instance, someone put a couch out on the street right across from Martine's building. Around noon a man and a woman got out of a station wagon, walked up to the couch, and started looking it over. They were both wearing white trousers, white shirts, and sunglasses. They looked elegant. The woman tested the springs. The man picked up a pillow and sniffed it. Who were they, couch inspectors?

The woman tried pushing the couch toward the car. The man just watched. She put her hands on her hips and said something. He shook his head. She made a fist. He made a face. Finally he got on the other end of the couch and helped her move it into the back of the station wagon. They tied it down. Then they both got in the car and drove away. End of story? I want to know what happened next! Where are they going with the couch? Are they still fighting over it? Will he ever sit on it? Sorry, you can't tune in tomorrow to find out!

Love, Toni

P.S. If you think you're living in a small place, you should see *this*. One step takes you from the couch to the chair, that's the living room. Another step to the table by the window, that's the dining room. A dive lands you on the futon. *Voilà!* Le bedroom.

P.P.S. I'm really eager for a letter from you. Please write and tell me everything!

"What did you do today?" Martine said when she returned at the end of the day.

"Not much."

"Did you go out?"

"No."

"You didn't go out? You stayed in all day? Well, I can't take you out now, Toni, I'm too tired."

Take her out? It sounded as if she were a dog Martine had to put on a leash. "I didn't ask you to do anything," Toni said.

"And if you did, I wouldn't," Martine said, giving herself the last word.

• CHAPTER •
THIRTEEN

Toni paced up and down the room. Somewhere in the building she heard a dog barking in a high, irritated voice. Poor thing! He'd been barking all morning. She knew what he was saying, because she was thinking the same thing. *Let me out! I'm alone! I'm a prisoner!*

She paced. Twenty steps from one end of the room to the other. She felt as if there were a clock ticking in her, ticking off the seconds, the minutes, the slow half hours, the impossibly long hours. *Tick tick tick tick tick ticktickticktick . . .*

She found three Devil Dogs in the freezer and devoured them. She wasn't hungry, just bored. Eating was something to do. Maybe she'd be so bored she'd finally gain weight. For about the twentieth time she looked at the clock. If she were home now, she'd be taking Paws's cat cookies from the cupboard. His after-breakfast treat. Would Mrs. Abish remember to feed him every day? Would she remember to pet him and talk to him? He could waste away from lack of affection. *Tick tick tick tick ticktickticktick . . .* Right about now, if she were home, she'd be getting ready to go down the street and collect Arnold. They'd go to the park and she'd answer his questions and follow him around. . . .

It would be hours before Martine returned. Hours before Toni would hear another human voice. She turned on the radio and the TV, put a record on the stereo and a cassette in the tape player. When everything was going full blast, she screamed at the top of her lungs.

She sat on the table eating potato chips. One of her father's favorite snacks. Would he return from Hertha Center slimmed down and eating rabbit food, things like celery and cucumbers? How were they retraining him? When he reached for a hot dog, did they slap his hand? Uh-uh-uh! Naughty, naughty! From now on, instead of coffee and a doughnut in the morning, would he be programmed to drink carrot juice?

She paced again. Up and down. She heard the dog barking again. His poor little hoarse voice! She listened intently. His message had changed. *Toni! Toni! Toni! Go out! Go out! Go Out!*

"I want to, but how can I?" she yelled. She went to the door. Three locks! At home they could go away for the day, and if they forgot to lock up, they wouldn't even worry. What if she went out and got mugged? Or lost? Or run over by one of the crazy drivers?

Go out! Go out! Go out!

She combed her hair and changed her shirt. She took the ring of keys off the bureau and tossed them from hand to hand. Well. Why not? She could always come right back. She unlocked the door. The hall was quiet. Only the prisoner dog yipped and yipped. "I wish I could take you out with me," Toni said. She went quickly down the hall and pressed the button for the elevator.

Outside, the heat fell on her, came around her like heavy arms. She was glad she was wearing only flip-flops, shorts, and a tiny shrink top. At the corner she looked back at Martine's building. Onward? Well . . . okay. She crossed a wide street on the WALK sign, hurrying as the sign flickered a red DON'T WALK and the cars snorted and inched forward impatiently. The sidewalk was chalky with heat and dust. Bits of paper lifted, fluttered, settled again in a brief gust of hot wind. She stared at a shoe in the gutter, a scarf. Who had they belonged to? Was someone walking around right now with one shoe?

She couldn't get used to how dirty the streets were. The wire baskets at the corners overflowed. But gradually she forgot that. It was the people she saw, people of every kind, every variety. A woman in a long red-and-gold African dress balanced a full shopping bag on her head. A group of men wearing orange hard hats sat in the shade of a building, eating their lunches. "Hi, honey," one of them said. Was he being friendly, or . . .? Before Toni could make up her mind, three boys swaggering toward her sent her hurrying to the side of the street. As they passed her, they broke into a song. A moment later, a man with a baby strapped to his chest danced in the middle of the sidewalk.

Toni walked on, looking into the windows of little stores, stopping to buy ice cream, then a magazine, later licorice. Her back was damp from the heat. The noise rose around her. *Dear Julie, What's my impression of New York? Noise, people, dirt, heat, people, noise, people, people, people!*

Back in Martine's building, she took the elevator up to

the fourth floor and walked down the hall. She stopped in front of a door but felt unsure if it was the right one. Was it 4L? Or 4N? Three locks, that was right. She went down to 4N. Three locks here, too. Every door had three locks! She looked up and down the hall, holding the keys.

Then the door at 4L opened. "Toni?" Martine said, stepping out. She had a glass in her hand. "What are you doing down there?"

Toni dropped the keys in her pocket and walked toward her sister.

"I thought I heard someone out here," Martine said. "Where've you been?"

"Out for a walk," Toni said. She held up her magazine.

"Out for a walk," Martine repeated, smiling faintly. She raised her glass to Toni. "You're becoming a regular New Yorker."

• CHAPTER •
FOURTEEN

August 30

Dear Julie,

This is my third day here. Martine has gone off to work. Even though being alone is not my favorite thing, it's better than being with her. Last night we almost had a fight after my parents called.

Martine answered the phone and talked to Dad for a few minutes. "Yes. . . . No. . . . Yes. . . . No" was what I heard of her side of the conversation. She sure doesn't put herself out to make talk, at least not for Dad. Anyway, she gave me the phone and Dad yelled, "Is that my Babyface?"

It was so great to hear his voice, Julie. He said the Hertha Center had him regimented. "You eat what they put in front of you and nothing else. You exercise when they tell you, even when you don't want to. And *no* bad habits. We even go to bed on schedule. This place reminds me of an Army camp with a wellness twist."

Then Mom got on and said, "Your father likes to complain, sweetie, but this is the best thing in the world for him." Julie, I got so homesick hearing Mom's voice, I almost lost it. I started saying, "Mom! Mom! Mom!" My sister looked over at me and gestured that she wanted to talk to Mom, so I handed her the phone. I said, "Let me talk to Mom again when you're done." Then I went to the bathroom, and when I came out, Martine was brushing her hair and the phone was hung up.

I said, "Martine, I told you I wanted to talk to Mom again!" It didn't bother her one bit. She just said, "Oh, yeah. There was a meeting or something. They said to say good-bye to Babyface." Then she gave me this weird, wrinkled-nose look, like she smelled something bad, and said, "Do they always call you that?"

I said, "No, not always."

She said, "Doesn't it bother you? Doesn't it bother you at all for them to call you Babyface? Doesn't it seem inappropriate to you for someone who's fourteen?" And she started talking about when she was fourteen, how mature she was, and blah blah blah *blah*.

I didn't want to hear it! I didn't want to hear how wonderful and *mature* she'd been at my age. I said, "Martine, what's so terrible about Mom and Dad having a nickname for me? They love me, that's why call me that."

Well, Julie, I definitely said the wrong thing! Martine practically spit out her next words. "And since they never had an *adorable nickname* for me, I suppose they didn't love me?"

I tried to explain that that wasn't what I meant. I said, "I'm the youngest, Martine, I guess that's why they do it." Julie, I made things worse!

Martine said, "What's so special about being the youngest?" Then she picked up her book and started reading, and when I tried to talk to her, she said, "I really don't feel like talking anymore." Boom! That was it. The queen doesn't want to talk, we don't talk! She brushed me off like I was a speck of dirt.

I went into her awful little dark kitchen just to get away from her. I drank a glass of ice water, then stood there, feeling the cold reaching my sinuses. I couldn't understand how my sister could be so rude, cold, and unloving. No, I did understand. She doesn't like me. She doesn't love me. I felt it from the first day. Julie, do you know how awful it is to be with someone who doesn't love you or even *like* you?

I was breathing hard. And listening. And waiting. What was I waiting for? For Martine to call me? To get me out of myself? To baby me? I knew it was totally absurd. I knew if I spent the rest of the night leaning against the sink and feeling like crud, it wouldn't bother Martine in the least. Oh, Julie, how I wished you were here! I know you, you would have helped me. You would have gone right up to Martine and said, "Listen, Martine, what's your problem? You don't like Toni? That's simply crazy! She's a wonderful person! Get real, Martine!" Well, Julie, just thinking that cheered me up enough to get me through the rest of the evening! Guess I'll sign off now and go out and mail this letter.

Love, Toni

August 31

Dear Julie,

This morning over breakfast, my sister and I had two conversations. First I asked if I was going to meet her boyfriend, Alex. She said he was away on vacation. "He went to Maine," she said. "I was supposed to go with him."

I said, "Why didn't you?" She gave me a long look and a small smile. "I'm sure you know, Toni." I said, "Because of me coming here?" No answer. I said, "I messed up your vacation." No answer.

In our second conversation she said, "Where are you going today?" I said, "Maybe to a movie." And she said, "Fine. See you later."

When she comes home later, we'll have more fascinating conversation. She'll say, "How was your day? Did you go out? Where'd you go?" I'll say, "Fine. Yes. To the movies."

She'll say, "Any problems?" I'll say, "No." She'll say, "Did you eat a good lunch?" I'll say, "Yes." She'll say "How about tonight, do you want to eat Greek? Japanese? Chinese? Or Ethiopian?" I'll say, "What do you think?" And she'll talk about each "cuisine." (Her word). She'll actually get happy-looking. We have our best conversations about food.

Love always,
Toni

P.S. I went into a bakery today to buy a corn muffin, and the guy behind the counter looked like L.R.'s double! I'm not kidding. He was even wearing a black T-shirt.

August 31

Dear Toni,

Yesterday I got your letter about the couch inspectors. Cute. Toni, doesn't it seem unbelievable that school is going to start in four days and neither one of us is going to be there? We have always started school together. I still don't really believe it's not going to happen this year.

My mother caught me taking a cigarette from her purse and she went bananas. "You're too young to smoke! I won't have my kids smoking, it's a rotten habit." Can you imagine, telling me to stop, when she's smoking worse then ever? But she had an answer to that, too. "I'm grown-up!" *Oh, really? Tell me about it.* That's what I wanted to say to her, but I bit my tongue. She was crying. First she yells, then she cries. First she makes me mad, then she makes me sorry for her.

Love,
Julie

September 1

Dear Julie,

Today I was walking through a park when I heard the most beautiful sound, something like rippling, ringing, chiming bells. The musician, a black man, was playing on what looked like two enormous silver bowls. Steel drums! It was the first time I ever saw them. He worked with mallets, rippling and tapping them over the inside of the bowls.

People slowed down to listen as they passed. Some stood around for a minute or two, then put down money and went on. I couldn't move. It was like being enchanted.

All the time the musician was playing, his face had this kind of enraptured look. I didn't think he even noticed me, but when he took a break, he asked if I wanted to try the drums! Yes! He showed me how to play melodies with a single mallet and chords with both mallets. He told me the steel drum was the national instrument of Trinidad. He said, "The heart must be clear for the music." I was so interested, I forgot about being nervous. I played the drums, Julie. I played them in public, and afterward I felt so wonderful.

Love,
Toni

P.S. Alex, my sister's boyfriend, called last night. She took the phone into the bathroom for privacy, but I could still hear her talking. It seems they were discussing when he was coming back. I heard Martine saying, "I can't wait . . . yes, she's leaving on the sixth!" Julie, I can understand why Martine will be glad to have her apartment to herself again, but did she have to sound so enthusiastic about my leaving? So very, very, *very* glad?

September 2

Dear Julie,

I've just spent the longest weekend of my life—with my sister. We did things together—we shopped, we did laundry, we ate, we saw a movie—and yet we're just as far apart as ever. I know she's marking time until I leave. Three more days. I can get through them, can't I, Julie?

Love,

Toni

P.S. I had my ears pierced Saturday. I've been wearing gold studs ever since. Martine hasn't even noticed.

• CHAPTER •
FIFTEEN

"Martine," Toni said, "I want to ask you something."

Martine lifted her eyes slowly from the magazine she was reading. "What?"

"Why do you dislike me?" Toni had been pretending to read for the past hour but had been brooding all the while.

Martine's eyebrows went up. Amusement? Disbelief? "Where do you get that idea?"

"From everything you do and everything you say."

"Everything I say?" Martine repeated. "I don't recall ever saying any such thing about you."

"I don't mean in so many words. I mean . . . attitude. Remember when you said I kept you from going on vacation with Alex?"

"I did not say that."

"You implied it. That's what you meant."

"Oh, now, wait a minute, I don't agree with that, but even if I did, what has that got to do with my liking or not liking you?"

"Martine, I know it's been a rotten week for you. I'm here. You can't do anything without having to think about me. I had to come because of Daddy, but that doesn't mean you like it. Or me."

"Why are you saying all this?" Martine put down the magazine. "What's going on here, Toni?"

Toni's eyes suddenly filled. "I can't stand how cold you are to me. We've been sitting here for one hour without a single word. And it's like that every night. I just made up my mind I had to say something. Maybe it's stupid of me. I'm going home in a couple of days, I didn't have to say anything."

"I'll agree with that," Martine said.

Toni bit her lip. She didn't have anything definite to go on, it was all feeling, intuition, instinct. Could she trust that? What if Martine was this way with everyone? But she couldn't be, Toni reasoned, or how would she have any friends?

"You know, just the way you look at me," Toni said, more bravely than she felt, "and the way you *don't* look at me, makes me feel disliked by you."

"Look at you, don't look at you . . . What does that mean, Toni? Isn't that rather vague? I thought you were intelligent. What are you doing, plucking things out of the air this way? You're creating a problem, is that it? Are you bored?"

If not for her sister's tiny, sarcastic smile, Toni might have backed off then. "Why do you take out your feelings on me?" she said. "What did I ever do to you?"

Martine stared. "I don't—"

"You do," Toni said.

"Well, if I do—" Martine bit her lip. "If I do that, I apologize," she said stiffly.

"You're giving me that cold smile again. You don't take anything I say seriously. You treat me like I'm not real, not a real person."

Martine sat up straight. "I'm not the one who treats you that way! It's Mom and Dad who do that. My point exactly about that awful nickname. Babyface," she said scornfully. "Is that you?"

Toni's eyes smarted. At that moment she wanted to be home so much, she could hardly stand it. *Don't cry,* she ordered herself. *Do not cry.* Deep down, she must have been hoping Martine would deny everything, that she would swoop her up in a hug and say, "Toni! Of course I like you. I *love* you! You're my sister, aren't you?"

But what Martine did was look up and say, "So you think I never liked you?" She fingered the pages of her magazine. "Well, who knows, you just might be right."

• CHAPTER •
SIXTEEN

Later that night Toni awoke to find Martine shaking her. Shadowy light from the street made dark, menacing shapes of the furniture, and her sister, her hair wild and snaky, loomed over Toni. "Wake up," she said. "Wake up."

"What time is it?" Toni mumbled.

"One, two, I don't know. What does it matter, I haven't been able to sleep. I want to talk to you."

Toni pushed aside the sheets. She didn't know anything she'd want to hear from Martine, or anything she'd want to say to her, except that she hated her, and this was the rottenest time she'd ever had in her life, and maybe she would like to kill her. "I've got to pee," she said, and fled into the bathroom.

She sat down on the closed toilet seat. She didn't turn on the light. Maybe she'd stay there all night. Not come out until morning. Outside, a siren wailed. Toni bent over with her head on her knees. She'd sleep right here.

"Toni?" Martine was knocking on the door. "What are you doing in there?"

"None of your business," Toni mumbled.

Martine knocked on the door again. "Come out, please."

Toni opened the door. "What do you want?"

"I told you, I want to talk to you."

"In the middle of the night? What about?"

"Our talk, last night—it's kept me awake for hours."

"Did it? I'm glad," Toni burst out. She went back to the bed and slid under the sheet on her side.

"This business of me not liking you—have you got it in your head that I'm jealous of you?" Martine said. "Is that the story? That I'm the jealous older sister, and because of that I don't like you? Is that what's underneath all that whining? If so, forget it, I'm not jealous."

"I don't whine," Toni protested. "And I didn't say anything about jealousy." She sat up. "Anyway, you agreed, you said it yourself. You said you didn't like me. I didn't make up a story. Why are you doing this now? I was sleeping! I want to go back to sleep. Why can't you leave me alone?"

"Let me remind you that you started this, Toni."

"So what if I did? I want to end it. I don't even want to be here. Two more days and I'm going home, and you can forget about me for the rest of your life!"

"Calm down."

"I am calm. You calm down!"

Martine sighed. "Look, this is getting out of hand. Let's both be calm. Can you hear this? I am not jealous."

"I never said you were."

"And I do not *not* like you."

"You do not *not?*"

"That's right, I do not *not.* I do not *not* like you. Okay?"

What was she supposed to do now? Agree with Martine

like a doormat, no matter what her eyes and ears and brains told her? "It's okay with me," she said. "You can say anything you want. I still think you don't like me."

"Oh, hell." Martine slid down in the bed.

There was silence. The refrigerator clicked on. The air conditioner hummed. Otherwise, silence.

Toni closed her eyes. She and her sister were lying only inches apart, but they might as well have been on separate continents.

"This place is too damn hot," Martine said suddenly.

Was that her fault, too? This apartment was too small for two people. It was a little torture box! She pushed the sheet off her shoulders and lay still, very still. Through the walls she could hear the elevator—a gusty, hollow sound, like wind at the shore. If only she were at the shore . . . the sun . . . sand . . . cool water on her feet . . . Julie said, *Look at the waves, Toni!* There was a crash, and Toni opened her eyes. Martine was talking.

Her voice rattled like pebbles in Toni's ear. "This notion of yours that I don't like you. Give me evidence. Give me something solid, not just this wimpy, boo-hoo you-don't-like-me stuff."

"You don't kiss," Toni said.

"What? I don't kid?"

"That, too. But what I said was kiss. *Kiss.*" Toni sat up. She could feel the heat rising off her skin. "When you kiss, you kiss air."

"What are you talking about?" Martine said.

"And you don't hug," Toni went on doggedly. "You never touch me. When you call Mom, you don't talk to me. When you come home, we never do anything together. You don't care about me. You don't even know I exist."

"Oh, I know you exist, all right. I can't overlook your existence." Martine laughed briefly. "But, listen, do you think relations between people are a one-way street? What about you? When did I ever hear you say, 'Martine, let's do something'?"

"You wouldn't want to if I did."

"Maybe I wouldn't," she said coolly. "But did you ever ask? And another thing, you're making me out to be this cold person, and I resent it. I know I'm not the most demonstrative person in the world, but that's not a crime. Alex understands. He says that for me, holding hands is an emotional thing. That's the way I am. I'm reserved."

"I'm not," Toni said in a hoarse voice. "I'm emotional."

"Well, good for you. That and a dollar fifteen will get you a ride on the subway."

"And Mom and Dad aren't that way, either. They like to hug and kiss."

"Really? What makes you so sure of that?"

"Because I live with them, Martine." Toni hated this. She hated fighting. How had she gotten into this mess?

"I know you think you're an expert on our parents," Martine said, "but did it ever occur to you that there are things you don't know about them? Tell me, when was the last time you saw them hugging?"

What was Martine getting at? What *things* wouldn't Toni know about her parents? Nothing, she told herself. As for them hugging, she wanted to spit out her answer: "They hug all the time, for your information!" But it wasn't true, and when she tried to remember the last time she'd seen them even touching hands, she couldn't. And for some odd reason her heart began to thud under her ribs.

Martine was talking again, in a low voice, almost as if to herself. "When I was your age, I could hardly wait to get away from home. It was so awful. I thought everything would be terrific if I could just get away from them." She was bent over her upraised knees. "And then, when I did get away, when I went to college, it wasn't terrific there, either." She spoke so softly, Toni had to turn to hear her. "I didn't have anyone to depend on, no one but me," Martine said. "And that's the way it's been. No one but me. . . . I did everything for myself. It's hard. It's hard being alone, knowing there's nobody you can turn to."

"You had Mom and Dad," Toni said. She felt scooped out, breathless. That awful thudding under her ribs wouldn't stop.

"Did I?" In the dim glow from the street, Martine's eyes were just darkness. "You think I had Mom and Dad? It didn't seem that way to me. It seemed to me they had all they could do just to keep their own problems under control."

What problems? What did she mean? What was she talking about? What was so *awful* at home that she *had* to get away? "I don't understand," Toni said. "I don't know what you're talking about."

Martine got up and moved restlessly around the room in her bare feet, finally lighting on the windowsill. "It's cooler here," she remarked. She looked out. "Do you believe it, the dog patrol is out in the park at this hour."

Toni didn't want to hear about dogs. "What were you saying about Mom and Dad?"

Martine didn't answer for a moment. Then, "Nothing," she said. "If you don't know . . ."

"If I don't know what?"

"They've kept you in ignorance," she said. "I knew they would. That was part of their agreement."

Toni couldn't make sense out of anything she was hearing. She waited for more, but Martine was silent and soon got back in bed and pulled the sheet up to her chin. "Listen, I've said too much. You don't know about these things, and maybe that's just as well. Who am I to disturb the universe? . . . Let's go to sleep. I have to work tomorrow."

A growl came out of Toni, and she bit the pillow.

"What are you doing?" Martine said.

"I don't know. Having a fit! You started telling me something and then you stopped. I hate being treated like a dumb kid."

"Did you ever hear of Pandora, the one who opened the box she was told to leave alone? Leave it alone, Toni."

"Why should I? You made it sound like something awful was happening at home, you said you couldn't wait to get away from Mom and Dad. Why? Why do you make it sound like they did something horrible to you? Tell me what you mean."

"Do you really want to know?" Martine said.

"Yes," Toni said, and her heart began that awful thumping again.

"Well, Toni, you think there's just one Mom and Dad, but I know something else. Mom and Dad changed their style when you came on the scene. No more talk about divorce, no more arguing. Not in front of the baby! Sure, it was okay for *me* to sit in my room and shake when they got going, that never stopped them. But they stopped for you."

"Stopped what?" she said. "What do you mean, 'when they got going'?"

"Fighting," Martine said flatly. "Didn't you hear me?"

"Mom and Dad fighting?" There was an impulse in Toni to laugh in her sister's face, and yet she felt sick and scared. What was she going to hear?

"When I was fourteen, they broke up," Martine said. "They'd had another big quarrel and Dad slugged Mom. It was the straw that broke the camel's back."

Toni swung around. "What did you say?" Was Martine crazy? Her father slapping her mother? No, not slapping—*slugging*. "Dad, you're talking about Dad? He never touched Mom, never in his whole life." Her voice was firm, but her lips felt loose, wobbly. "He wouldn't do that. He's not that kind of person. And Mom wouldn't let herself be hit! She wouldn't stay with Dad for one moment—"

"Exactly. That's why she finally decided to get a divorce."

It was all too bizarre. Fights? Splitting? Divorce? Martine could have been talking about Julie's parents. "I don't believe you," Toni said breathlessly.

"You think I'm lying? No, Toni. I saw it. We were in the kitchen. I saw Dad do it. He hit Mom, hit her hard enough for her to fall. And get a bloody mouth. And then he threw a chair down on the floor and kicked it." Martine was talking in a monotone now. "I picked the chair up. I don't know why I did it. Then he left. Mom started peeling carrots and crying and saying she was going to leave him."

Toni's heart was beating wildly. "You don't cry when you peel carrots. That's onions."

"He moved out," Martine said. "I don't know how long he was gone. Maybe a month. I remember how big the house felt with him gone. And how quiet. I was glad. He got a room at the YMCA. One day he came to the house to get his clothes. Mom wasn't home, but I was. He got his stuff and left. Then, maybe a month later, Mom found out she was pregnant. And he came back. They stayed up all one night, talking. Talking, talking, talking. I was in my room. I could hear them all night long, talking. I remember being scared that they were going to start fighting. But they didn't. And it was after that they bought the house on Oak Street."

"Our house?" Stupid question, Toni thought, but she was in a state of shock. Was Martine telling the truth? Had her father really hit her mother? *Slugged* her? Hit her hard enough to knock her to the floor?

"Mom told me they were having a new start. They were putting aside their differences. None of us was ever going to talk about the past again. And we didn't. The idea was to protect the baby. Keep the baby innocent. Pretend everything is okey-dokey. In other words, lie, lie, lie."

Toni sank down in the bed. "I just can't believe it," she said. "I just can't believe that about Dad."

Once Toni had read a book where the heroine would look at the clock every time something happened to her. *Two-ten,* she'd think, *I'll remember this moment forever.* If she got a splinter, she would look at the clock. *Six-fifteen, I'll remember this moment forever.* If she forgot her locker key: *Nine-twenty, I'll remember this moment forever.* It was silly and funny.

Toni looked at the clock. *Two-twenty-four, I'll remember this moment forever.* Only this wasn't silly, and it wasn't funny.

• CHAPTER •
SEVENTEEN

Wednesday, the last night of Tony's stay, Martine came home from work wired up and talking fast. "It was a zoo at work today. I need a corner to stand in and scream. Toni, get out of those jeans. We're going out to eat."

"We can order in," Toni said. They'd done that a few nights.

"No, I don't want to eat in or order in. It's your farewell dinner. Let's do it right. Hurry up, get dressed. Alex is calling later, I have to be back for that."

Toni put on a skirt and blouse. She combed her hair and looked at herself in the bathroom mirror. Was she possibly the same person she'd been ten days ago? How could she be? Ever since the night Martine had told her about their parents she had been walking around as if in a dream. *Mom. Dad. Who are you, really? Who am I?*

Outside, the sidewalks steamed. It had rained earlier. They walked to a restaurant in Little Italy, crossing Houston Street on the way. "Why is the name of a Texas city on a New York street?" Toni asked. She didn't care, but she felt the need to talk, to say something, to keep her thoughts at bay.

"I don't know, but you say it 'how-stun' to rhyme with 'wow-fun.' "

The restaurant was five steps down from the sidewalk. There were half a dozen tables covered with blue-checked cloths. Everything was simple and plain, except the prices. Toni read the right-hand side of the menu. "This place is expensive."

"Don't worry about it, the food is great. Relax."

Relax! Martine was a fine one to talk. Even the way she ate was tense, eating rapidly and sighing between bites of the veal parmigiana. But finally she leaned back, tipping her head up toward the ceiling, and said, "I have to learn to let the job go. I am learning. It's gone." She wiped her hand across her face and sat there with her eyes closed, taking deep breaths. She opened her eyes and smiled. "So, Toni. Tomorrow you go home."

Toni nodded. "I packed today. I didn't do much else."

"You should have gone to a movie or something, done one last New York thing."

"I went to a movie yesterday."

"Oh, I didn't know."

Toni mentioned the name of the movie. Her napkin slipped to the floor and she bent to pick it up. When she straightened up, she took a breath and said, "Martine, you didn't know about the movie because you didn't ask me anything about my day."

"Do I have to ask everything? Why didn't you tell me?"

Toni bit her lip. There was always an answer from Martine. Maybe she was right, but how do you tell things to someone who doesn't seem interested?

They had iced tea, spumoni, and cookies for dessert. They chatted, wary with each other, or so it seemed to Toni, sticking to safe subjects like the weather and the food. Then, nibbling a cookie, Martine looked across at Toni and said, "So, have you thought at all about the things I told you about Mom and Dad?"

Toni held the frosty glass against her cheek. She nodded.

"And—?"

"I don't know. It's—I don't know. I hate to think about it. Dad hitting Mom." The moment she said the words, her lips felt numb. It was too horrible to think about.

"I remember when Dad came back home . . . from living at the Y? I felt so mixed up, confused," Martine said. "I was relieved in one way, because I didn't want my parents to be divorced. But I couldn't see them as the happy couple. They were covering up. They were pretending everything that had happened *hadn't* happened. You want to hear this?"

"I guess so," Toni said. She pushed back from the table, put space between Martine and herself.

"They sleep in twin beds, right? That's when they got them. They stuck their marriage together. It was coming apart, and they patched it up, glued it together. Moving was part of it. New home. Like putting a new cover on a book. But what if it's the same old book inside?"

"But they weren't fighting anymore."

"True. But you know how they managed that? They didn't talk to each other all that much. New marriage, new home, new baby. No talk . . . I didn't want to move. I liked where we lived. I had my friends, my school, I grew up there. They didn't ask me, though, just went ahead and did it. They turned *my* life inside out to solve *their* problems. They didn't think about me. All they thought about was themselves—and you."

All they thought about was themselves. Wasn't that a perfect description of Julie's parents? Toni shifted in her seat. "Where did you live before?"

"Sunnyfield Avenue in the city." Martine stirred her tea. "On the west side. It was such a great street. Lots of nice little houses and trees. We lived on the side of a hill."

Toni tried to imagine that other house, that other life, her sister as a teenager, a girl like her. A girl sitting in her room, listening to her parents fighting.

"You know what's so weird right now?" Martine said. "Just talking about it is making me feel awful all over again, like the whole thing is happening again in big living color." She looked down, biting her lip. Her eyes filled.

"Martine . . ." Toni's hand went out, covered her sister's hand.

They stayed that way for a minute, then Martine withdrew her hand. "I'm okay." She wiped her eyes with her napkin. "Thanks. You want to ask me anything?"

"There's one thing I don't understand."

Martine nodded, as if she knew what Toni was going to say and approved. Martine, who had never approved of anything about Toni before! But something had changed between them. In that moment when they sat with their hands laced together, something had shifted, some connection had been made that hadn't been there before.

Toni fiddled with the salt shaker. "If Mom and Dad hated each other, why did she get pregnant?"

"I didn't say they hated each other, Toni. I never said that. I said they quarreled, they fought, they yelled."

Quarreled. Fought. Yelled. Another definition of the Jensens, the immature ones who didn't think about their kids, who didn't know anything about getting along. But now it was her parents, too.

"Besides," Martine said, "people can fight and still go to bed. That's not so unusual."

Toni nodded as if she'd always known that. "But it was worse than fighting. You said he slap—slug—" She felt that racing of her heart and couldn't get the words out. And thought: Julie's father never hit her mother, which meant that *her* father was rungs below Mr. Jensen on the moral ladder. This hit her like a shock of cold water. "Do you hate Dad, Martine?" she blurted.

Her sister's shoulders tensed. "Maybe." Then she shook her head quickly. "No, I don't, not anymore. I've never felt the same toward him again, though. Sometimes I forget all about it . . . and then I remember. And it horrifies me. It makes me feel sick and disgusted. I can't stand the thought of one person hitting another. I can't stand the thought of a man using his strength to bully a woman. When I think of Mom hitting the floor—"

Toni's eyes blurred, the room seemed to rock around her. She had a vision of her mother on the floor, of herself bending over her mother, then turning to scream and spit at her father.

• CHAPTER •
EIGHTEEN

"Fourteen dollars," the cabdriver said, turning off the meter and stopping in front of the house.

Toni pawed through her pocketbook. "Fourteen?" All she had was a ten-dollar bill and a handful of change. The driver put her arm over the back of the cracked vinyl seat and turned to watch her. Flustered, Toni said, "I don't have enough money."

"I knew this was going to happen," the cabbie said gloomily. She had straight blond hair, a pockmarked face. "I had a feeling in my gut all the way out here."

"I can give you my name. I can get the money tomorrow. I'll pay you, I promise."

"Isn't there anybody home you can get money from *now?*"

Toni shook her head. Her parents wouldn't be home until later this evening, around nine o'clock.

The cabbie pushed some buttons, and the radio crackled with static and incomprehensible words. "Fifty-two. I've got a stiff on Oak Street," the driver said into the speaker. "Roger. Over."

Toni felt stupid and slightly frightened. What was going to happen now? Was this a crime? Would they call the police? Slow down, she told herself. You can go across the street and borrow from Mrs. Abish, or down the block to Mrs. Frankowitz.

"Bleeegh somebody bleeegh bleeegh . . . in the bleegh?" the radio voice growled.

"Negative. What do I do?"

More growling, sounding even more menacing. Meanwhile, with a surge of relief, Toni remembered that her mother always kept emergency money in the desk in the living room. She tapped the driver on the shoulder. "Wait, wait, I can get it. I just remembered—" She opened the door. "I'll only be a minute. I'll be right back."

"I ain't moving," the driver said.

Toni ran up the walk to the house. Their lawn was dry and yellow. She glanced over at the Jensens'. Everything was quiet, the whole street was quiet, eerily quiet, and empty. She unlocked the front door. The cabbie was leaning out the window on her arm, watching. Toni waved reassuringly and went in.

The house was dim, the shades drawn. "Hello . . . ?" she breathed into the emptiness. Nothing moved. Nothing responded. What had she expected?

The desk drawer was stuck and didn't want to open. "Open!" Toni ordered, and gave it a sharp tug. The drawer flew open. Inside was an envelope with three twenties.

When she paid the cabbie, Toni remembered to give her a tip. And the cabbie remembered to give Toni a smile. "I knew you were going to come through," she said.

"I have an honest face," Toni joked.

"Yeah, I can tell these things," the cabbie said seriously. She pushed in the clutch. "I know things about people."

"Do you?" Toni held on to the window for a moment. Did this woman know things other people didn't? Was she wise? Toni leaned toward her. There was so much she needed to know. *Tell me about my parents. . . . Tell me how they could have done the things Martine said and yet be the people I think they are. . . . Tell me how I can keep on loving them. . . .*

That morning, in the cab Martine had flagged outside her building, they had both been quiet, barely talked on the way to the bus terminal. Martine, in a sleeveless dress, fragrant with perfume and lip gloss, had alternately looked out the window and tapped her fingers restlessly on her pocketbook. "I'm going to be late to work," she said once.

"Sorry," Toni said.

"No, it's all right."

At the bus station, part of Toni had wanted to stand aside from Martine, to show her independence. And part of her had wanted to throw her arms around her sister. Martine had settled it by kissing Toni, her version of a kiss, her cool cheek against Toni's, her lips kissing air.

In the house again, Toni stood in the front hall and listened. No horns, no sirens, no buzz-moan-whine of the city. It was so quiet! Negative noise. The quiet had a hum of its own.

She went through the house, opening windows. The two beds in her parents' room were stripped, quilts folded at the bottom. Toni remembered now all the nights her parents hadn't even slept in the same room, her father going to the couch in the family room. "I was restless last night," he would say in the morning, meeting her in the hall. "Poor Daddy," she'd say, and lean against him for a moment. That was all. She had never thought about it. Had she thought about *anything?*

She got linens from the hall closet, snapped out the sheets, and began to spread them over the beds; but a wave of revulsion, a sour heaviness in her stomach, stopped her. She left the sheets piled at the foot of the beds.

Everything in the house seemed strange until she went into her own room. She touched the bed, the desk, the dressing table. Her Bobby McFerrin poster was peeling off the wall, and she taped it on again. She picked up a book she'd been reading when she left, then rearranged the stuffed animals on the shelf. Paws had slept on her bed. She saw hairs and the indent of his body.

In the kitchen, she discovered that the clock over the stove was dead. It had been making gaspy noises for weeks. She got up on the step stool and took the clock off the wall. It left a pale, round space. The hands had stopped at eight-ten. Did that mean anything? She held the clock for a moment. They'd had it for years. When she was little, she thought it was alive, that its cheerful face watched her approvingly when she ate.

Paws still hadn't shown up. She stood at the back door and called him. The leaves on the plum tree rattled gently. What if something had happened to Paws? She dialed Mrs. Abish's number, but there was no answer. She called Julie's number next. Suppose, despite the closed, blank look of the house, Julie was actually home. Suppose she answered the phone: "Toni! Surprise! I'm home, and I've been waiting for you!"

She let the phone ring a dozen times, then hung up. Her hand was barely off the receiver when it rang. She picked it up, and Julie's name rushed out of her mouth. "Julie!"

"Toni?" her sister said. "Did you just get in? How was your trip home?"

"It was okay, but I didn't have enough money for the cab."

"You should have told me you were short," Martine said. "What did you do?"

"I took care of it."

"Are Mom and Dad home yet?"

"Not till nine o'clock."

"Oh, right." A pause. Then: "Toni? There's something I want to tell you. A couple of things."

Toni held the phone away from her ear. Was Martine going to come up with another unpleasant story about their parents?

"I've been thinking, all the stuff we talked about . . . I hope you remember that it's all history. You know what I mean? It happened a long time ago. Try to remember that. Will you keep that in mind?"

"If it's ancient history, Martine, why does it still hurt you so much?"

"Oh, I'm all over it," her sister said.

Are you? Toni thought.

"And the other thing—I don't know if I said this or not, but I don't want you to forget that I'm your sister."

"I'm not likely to."

"No, listen. This isn't clowning around."

No kidding. When did Martine ever clown around?

"What I'm trying to say is, if you need me for anything, I'm here. I'm always here. I'm your sister and I'm always here for you."

"Well," Toni said after a moment. "Thank you, Martine."

Late that afternoon, her mother called. "Brace yourself, sweetheart, we're not coming home tonight. In fact, we're not coming home until Monday night."

Toni's palms went damp. "Are you fighting?" Her voice was rough, blurry.

Her mother misunderstood. "Friday? No, not Friday. Monday we'll be home."

"Monday?"

"What'd you say, sweetie? I can't hear you too well. Is the connection all right on your side? Can you hear me?"

"The connection is fine," Toni said, speaking more directly into the receiver. *The connection is fine.* The words echoed in her head. No. The connection was not fine. The connection was frayed, suspect.

"I'm sorry to do this to you, sweetie, but there's a special program on affirmative thinking, and we were strongly advised to stay for it."

"Okay."

"I would have called you sooner, but it only came up at the last minute. We just found out about it this morning, too late to call you at Martine's. Now, what I've been thinking is that you could stay with Mrs. Abish across the street."

"Mom, I don't have to do that."

"That way my mind will be at rest," Toni's mother went on. "I'll call her as soon as I hang up with you and make the arrangements."

"Mom." Toni raised her voice. "Mom, listen. I want to stay here. I want to stay in my own house."

There was a short silence. Then her mother said, "Do you think you can handle it?"

"Mom. Yes!"

"There's no food—"

"I'll go to the store."

"Do you have any money?"

"There's the emergency money in your desk. I'll use that."

"That drawer sometimes gets stuck. You have to—"

"Jiggle it around to get it open," Toni finished. "I know, Mom. I did it."

Her mother laughed a little uncertainly. "Well, you do seem to have everything figured out. You'll go to school tomorrow, so you'll only really be alone over the weekend. Four days—Friday, Saturday, Sunday—"

"Mom," Toni interrupted, "I know the days of the week."

"I'll call every night," her mother said.

"You don't have to do that. I'll be all right."

Her father got on the phone. "We don't have to do this program, Babyface. It's optional."

"Mom said the program is important, so I think you should stay." Her voice rose. "And please don't call me Babyface."

He didn't seem to have heard her. "Brave of you to stay alone," he said. "I'm proud of you."

What was so brave about a fourteen-year-old girl staying

in her own house for a few days? Why was everything she did such a huge deal to him? To both of them? Why were they stupefied every time she did something the least bit independent? Martine hadn't acted that way. In fact, the opposite—she had expected Toni to do everything for herself.

Later she put a frozen pizza in the oven, and while it was heating, she stood in the doorway, calling Paws. He appeared around the side of the garage and picked his way across the yard toward her, mewing and talking the whole distance. "Paws!" She scooped him up and kissed his little face. Here was somebody who didn't worry about her, who accepted her as she was, as she had been, and as she would be. He flattened himself against her body and began a slow, heavy hum of happiness.

• CHAPTER •
NINETEEN

"You weren't in school yesterday . . . or the day before," Mrs. Evelyn said, looking at Toni over the tops of her half glasses.

"I know," Toni said. She leaned on the counter in the office. She had just finished explaining the whole situation to Mrs. Evelyn.

"Nobody answered your phone at home," Mrs. Evelyn went on.

"Nobody was there. My parents are in Ohio," she said again.

"And you were—?"

"In New York City." Behind her, Toni heard the office door open.

"New York City?" Said as if Toni had mentioned the moon.

"Yes. Could you tell me what my room assignment is please, Mrs. Evelyn? And give me my schedule?"

"Just one minute, young lady. I'll get to everything. And what do *you* want?" Mrs. Evelyn said, looking past Toni.

Toni turned. L.R. Faberman was standing just behind

her. Same L.R., dark glasses and all. Maybe a little bit taller, but maybe she was a bit taller, too. She hoped so. She was just about looking him in the eye.

"I forgot my locker key," L.R. said. Had his voice been that deep when she had talked to him at the drugstore? He was wearing flowered shorts and what seemed to be the same black T-shirt he'd worn all last year.

"You forgot something else, too," Mrs. Evelyn said.

L.R. pushed his dark glasses up on his nose. "No. Just my locker key."

"You forgot your pants," she said.

He looked down at his bare legs. So did Toni. Nice.

"And *you* forgot your written excuse," Mrs. Evelyn said to Toni.

"I can't bring it until my parents come home. Tuesday I'll bring it in." Toni wondered if she should tell Mrs. Evelyn again about her father's heart attack and the Hertha Center.

"And who's home with you now? Are you alone?"

"I . . . no. I have someone with me." Toni didn't say it was a cat. She glanced at L.R., then at the clock. "The bell's going to ring, Mrs. Evelyn. I hope I'm not late for my first class."

"Me, too," L.R. said.

Mrs. Evelyn opened a drawer. Slowly. She pulled out a folder. Slowly. Nothing could rush her. If there had been an earthquake, if the building had been shaking, if the room had been on fire, she would have moved in the same deliberate way. She went to her desk and began typing. Slowly. L.R. and Toni looked at each other. He put his finger to his temple like a gun.

Mrs. Evelyn came back and gave L.R. a key on a leather

thong. "Use that and return it immediately. Are you going to forget your locker key again?"

"I hope not," he said.

"What kind of an answer is that?"

"Honest."

Toni hid a little smile as Mrs. Evelyn put down her locker key and a pass card. "Do I have to tell you about locker keys?" she said. "The rules?" Toni shook her head. Mrs. Evelyn took a sheet of paper from the folder. "This is your schedule."

"Is this all I need, then?"

"All you need?" Mrs. Evelyn said. "Your wits would help. It would help all you kids. But God forbid you should bring them to school. Why are you still here?" she said to L.R. "Go!"

In the hall, L.R. went one way, Toni the other. She wondered if he remembered that they'd talked in the drugstore.

All day people kept asking, "Where were you? Where's Julie? How are you going to survive without her?"

"I swear I've never seen you without Julie," Kelly Lutz said in gym. Her hair was pink again.

"It's the first time I've ever started school without her."

"You were always her shadow," Kelly said. "Or is it the other way around?"

Friday afternoons after school were always zooey. Kids screamed and rushed through the halls in a crazed way. Julie and Toni always had, too. But that afternoon, while everyone else lunged for lockers and doors, Toni walked slowly down the stairs, thinking about the weekend, making plans. She opened her locker, knelt, and took out a stack of books, trying to decide what to take home.

"Hi," someone said. It was L.R., opening a locker two down from her. "What homeroom did you get?" he asked.

"Twenty-four. Mr. Bentson."

"Aha! I hear he's a terror on attendance. Do you have trouble getting up in the morning on time?"

Toni shook her head.

"I do," L.R. said. "I'm glad I got Ms. Crandall."

"Room twenty-seven."

L.R. nodded. "She is very cool. . . . I still haven't returned the key to Evy-lion."

"Grrrrr," Toni said softly.

"She probably eats two or three my size for dinner every night."

Toni picked up her books. L.R. was cute. She'd have to remember to write Julie everything. She left school, crossed the street. She was at the corner when L.R. fell into step with her.

"Hi again," he said.

"Hi." Heat came up in her face.

"I just gave the key back to Evy-lion. I thought she'd be grateful, but she lectured me for not returning it this morning."

They walked to the next corner together. Now he would leave, Toni thought, but he kept walking with her. "Are you still working at Rite Bargain Drugs?" she said. How dull. She wanted to think of something more interesting to say.

"How do you know I worked there?" he asked.

"I saw you this summer. I came through your line."

His dark glasses stared blankly at her. "You did?"

She was a little taken aback by his surprise. It would have been nice if he remembered her. "We talked," she said.

"Oh . . . maybe I remember."

Maybe he remembered. How flattering. Well, he must have waited on a million people. Why should she expect him to remember her out of them all? But somehow she did.

"What'd we talk about?" he said.

"Not too much. I mentioned that we went to the same school."

"You know, I think I do remember, now that you say it."

Did he? Or was he just being nice?

"I'm not working there anymore," he said. "My father doesn't like me to work during the school year. Anyway, it was just a summer job."

"Did you like the boss?" Toni asked.

"She was all right."

"I think she's excellent." She smiled down into her books.

"You know Violet?"

"Oh, yes. Her name is Violet Chessmore. Right?"

"Right."

"She lives on the same street I do."

"Oh, that's another coincidence," he said.

"What's the first one?"

"Our lockers being so close together."

"And there's a third coincidence," Toni said, trying not to laugh. "Chessmore's my name, too."

He gave her another one of those blank, dark-glasses looks.

"Violet's my mother," she said lamely.

"Violet is your mother?" He sounded almost as doubtful as Mrs. Evelyn this morning.

"I'm Toni Chessmore. I guess I should have told you right away. Sorry. I thought you'd like the joke."

"I did," he said. "You really strung me along. I'm L.R. Faberman."

She bit her lip so she wouldn't say *I know your name.* He stuck out his hand and they shook. His hand was damp, or was it hers?

"Now that we're really introduced," he said, "do you mind if I ask you something? Are you new in school?"

"Me? I've lived in Ridgewood my whole life."

"I haven't lived anywhere my whole life. My family used to live in Carbondale, in Pennsylvania. Then we moved to Scranton. Then my father and I moved to Binghamton. Then we came here. I'm new here. Or I was, last term."

I know! She bit her lip again. "Why did you think I was new?" she asked.

"I didn't."

"Oh, but you asked—"

"I guess I was hoping, sort of. You know, like 'the two new kids stick together' kind of thing?" She smiled, and he said, "Want to ask me something?"

"What?"

"Anything. Be my guest."

"Oh. Okay. Why do you wear dark glasses all the time?"

"My eyes are light-sensitive. Something I was born with." He pulled off the glasses and squinted at her. His eyes were a pale grayish-brown. "See, this really hurts me, and it's not even that sunny today." His face looked different without glasses, sweeter somehow.

"You wear them all the time?" she said.

"Except when I'm sleeping." He leaped for the branch of a tree and chinned himself half a dozen times, then dropped to the sidewalk. "I do a hundred pull-ups at home every day," he said.

She forgot to bite down on her lip. "And the pegboard in the gym at lunch."

"How do you know that? And don't tell me your father is the coach."

She looked up at the street signs, as if she'd never noticed them before. "This is where I turn," she said hastily. And she turned, and forgot to say good-bye.

• CHAPTER •
TWENTY

Toni was sitting on the back steps with Paws in her lap, brushing his coat, when the phone rang in the kitchen. She jumped up, dumping the cat. "Sorry," she apologized. With an offended look he began licking his shoulder.

The screen door slammed behind Toni. Eagerly she picked up the phone. Might be her mother, her sister, or even Mrs. Abish.

Yesterday after school Toni had gone over to visit. "Grraand to see you again." Mrs. Abish had fed Toni pound cake and milk laced with honey. Listening as Mrs. Abish talked, Toni wondered about Mr. Abish. Where was he? Oh, yes . . . dead. In the ground. She wondered if Mr. and Mrs. Abish had been happy, if they had ever quarreled. *Quarreled . . . fought . . . yelled . . . slugged. . .*

"Hello," Toni said now.

"Can I speak to Toni?"

"Speaking. Hello, L.R.," she said, not quite calmly.

"How'd you know it was me?"

"I recognized your voice."

"Oh. How'd you do that?"

"Don't know. Just did." She was smiling, her cheeks hot.

"You have an ear for voices."

"Wouldn't you recognize my voice?"

"I will, after this," he said.

Then they both fell silent.

"Umm, I—" she said finally.

"Well, there—" he said at the same moment.

"You go first," she said.

"No, you."

"No. You." She was firm, then surprised when he did.

"I was just going to say there aren't many Chessmores in the phone book. I only had to call one other number before this."

"Not many Fabermans, either," she said without thinking.

"How do you know that?" he asked.

And what was she supposed to say now? *Julie and I looked up all the Fabermans in the phone book?* They had done it months ago. "Oh, uh, I guessed," she said lamely. "I mean, isn't it an unusual name?"

"Sort of," he said. There was another silence, again broken by L.R. "Do you bowl, Toni?"

"I have, a few times."

"Did you like it?"

"I got a pretty low score. I'm not that great an athlete." That sounded sort of negative. "I'm a good singer, though." *That* sounded ridiculous! He hadn't asked about her singing voice.

"Are you in chorale?"

"No. But I might join this year." Really? That was a surprise to her, if not to L.R.

"What do you sing?"

"Soprano." She wiped her forehead. Why was she sweating? It wasn't that hot today.

"Do you think you'd like to bowl again sometime?"

"I might."

"Are you enthusiastic about that idea? Or negative? Or neutral?"

"What is this, a questionnaire?"

"The next question is . . . if you are enthusiastic, or even neutral, do you want to go bowling sometime? With me? Like tomorrow afternoon?"

"Oh!" She ran her hand over her forehead again.

"Does that mean yes?"

"It means . . . ahh . . . I'm thinking about it."

"Think fast! I like answers to my questions. No, I'm just teasing. Take your time."

"Well, um, I might like to." Would it be disloyal to Julie for her to go bowling with L.R.?

"That sounds like a yes. How about around two o'clock?"

"Two o'clock?" she repeated.

"Is something happening at two o'clock? You sound doubtful."

"I do? No, I was just—"

"Thinking about it," he finished for her.

"Right," she said weakly.

"We could go to the bowling alley in the mall. Do you know that place? Entertainment Plaza. Have you been there? They have pinball machines and pool tables. Do you play pool?"

"Yes. No. No," she said.

"Yes. No. No," he repeated. "You do know it, you haven't

been there, you don't play pool. I'll teach you sometime. Do you want me to teach you? Do you learn fast?"

"Yes. Yes," she said, enjoying herself, but still sweating.

"I bet you do," he said. "How do you usually get to the mall from your house, Toni?"

"I walk or ride my bike. Sometimes my mother drives me."

"So which one? Your mother, feet, or wheels? If it's feet, I could come to your house. Or I could meet you there."

Come to her house? Meet her there? He was way ahead of her. She hadn't even made her decision whether to go with him or not. But she was saved. "Toni," he said, "my father's calling me. Gotta hang up."

"Okay," she said. Relief. She could think it over, work it out in her mind.

But then he went on. "Two tomorrow afternoon at the mall, okay?"

"O . . . kay," she said, dragged into it, as she told herself immediately after hanging up. Immediately wondering what she had done. Wondering if Julie would be mad. Mad as a wet hen. Silly phrase. It went through her head several times as she ran up the stairs to check if she had anything good to wear for bowling. She shoved aside skirts, pants, blouses in her closet. Too small, too short, too juvenile! She and her mother had missed out on shopping, as usual, for new school clothes.

Toni ran downstairs again. She wouldn't go. She couldn't! Not because of clothes, not that superficial reason. She couldn't go bowling with L.R. because it would be too much like a date. Which would be wrong. It would create problems, upset Julie.

She got his number from information. Paws scraped himself along her leg. "Shh," she said. She dialed, but after two rings she hung up. How should she say this? She didn't want to hurt L.R.'s feelings. She should write it down. No, practice out loud.

She picked up Paws and looked into his blue Siamese eyes. "L.R., I'm sorry, but I can't go bowling with you. Are you wondering why? Well, L.R. . . ."

Paws wriggled in her arms.

"Please be patient, L.R. Let me explain this to you." She kissed his cool nose. "Well, L.R., you might remember that I mentioned my friend, Julie Jensen, to you when I saw you in the drugstore. And, well, you're Julie's! Well, not hers, exactly. She doesn't *own* you, but she loves you. Whereas I'm just—"

Paws' ears flattened against his head. He was getting ready to leap.

Toni held him firmly. "Patience, L.R., patience! I'm sure you want to know I'm *just what?* Just interested? Just curious? Just want to mess around with a boy a little?"

Paws squirmed out of her arms, landing on the floor with a thump.

"L.R.," Toni said reproachfully, "my intentions are pure. You don't have to run away from me!"

From beneath the table Paws eyed her, switching his tail. She knelt and took his face between her hands. "Now listen here, I'll go bowling with you. But what I'm going to do is tell you all about Julie. She's beautiful, you know. I'll show you her picture. You'll probably fall in love with her."

Paws suddenly grabbed Toni's fingers between his teeth, his way of letting her know that she was pushing him too far. Toni relaxed her hand until he unclenched his jaws. "Thank you, L.R. Just remember, this is not a date. Just a friendship thing."

Saturday night, Mrs. Frankowitz called to ask if Toni would take care of Arnold for a few hours the next morning. "Yes, sure," Toni said. They chatted for a few minutes, and Toni hung up reluctantly. The house seemed big and still at night. She stayed up late, reading, not eager to turn out the light. Then in the morning she overslept. When she saw the time, she raced through her shower and ate her breakfast standing in front of her closet, deciding what to wear.

"Something that's okay for baby-sitting *and* bowling," she said, out loud. Since she had no one to talk to, she talked to herself. She put her cereal bowl down on the bureau. "Shorts, my red shirt, a belt. Okay. That sounds good."

Twenty minutes later she knocked on the Frankowitz door. Mrs. Frankowitz answered with Arnold in her arms. "Arnold, here's Toni!" she cried, and bent her cheek toward Toni for a kiss. "How's your father, Toni?"

"Uh . . . good," Toni said awkwardly. She didn't want to talk about her father. "Arnold!" She put out her arms to the little boy, but he pulled away with a frown.

"Noooo," he said.

"What's the matter, old man?" Arnold's father appeared, a scarf wound around his throat, although it was a warm day. "Hello, Toni," he said. He held his head stiffly. "I strained my neck in the car." He pointed to the scarf. "Got a brace on under this. . . . Maybe Arnold doesn't want to go out," he said to his wife.

"Oh, yes, he does," Mrs. Frankowitz said.

"How do you know?" Mr. Frankowitz turned his head stiffly to look at his son.

"Oh, I know my boy," Mrs. Frankowitz said, smiling.

Toni watched the two of them. They seemed happy and to like each other. But was it true? It could be a pretense, a lie they made for the world—and Arnold.

"Arnold really missed you these past couple weeks, Toni," Mrs. Frankowitz said. "Didn't you, Arnold?"

"Nooooo."

"You want to go to the park with Toni this morning?"

"Nooooo."

"Sure you do, I know you do."

"Noooo. I don't vant to."

His father looked worried, but Mrs. Frankowitz put Arnold down and said, "Well, you're going, and you're going to have a wonderful time." Then, to Toni, "I think he's a little piqued that you went away. But he'll be all right."

She was right. Even though Arnold kept looking back at his house, once they went around the corner he became cheerful. "I vant to go to the park, Toni."

"Oh, you do?" she said. "That's a surprise."

"Yes, I vant to go there."

"I thought you didn't," she said.

"I do!"

"You want to go with me?"

"Yes, I vant to go with you."

"I don't know if I should take you," she teased. "You weren't nice to me. You didn't give me a kiss."

"I vill kiss you," he declared, and turned up his face.

She bent down and took his sweet, wet kiss. "Thank

you," she said. She gave him a kiss. "Now we'll go to the park."

"Yes, ve vill," he said.

L.R. was waiting outside the bowling alley for Toni, leaning back with one foot flat against the building. The moment she saw him, Toni thought, Why does he want to go bowling with me? Why do I want to go with him? What am I doing?

To gain time she knelt and retied her laces.

"Hi, Toni." L.R. had seen her. "Good timing, I jud god here."

"What's the matter?" she said. First Mr. Frankowitz, now L.R.

He blew his nose. "I god a code. Don't ged too close."

"Is it a hard code to crack?" Bad, baaad joke, but he laughed. Nice, nice boy.

"I ged these things aboud three times a year, Toni. They come on jud like that." L.R. snapped his fingers. "I woke up thid morning thid way. My father wanted me to stay home, but I said no way, I didn't want to stay home, not today."

In the bowling alley they rented shoes. "You want to keep score?" L.R. asked.

"I don't know if I remember how."

"Here, I'll show you." Leaning on the desk, looking at the score sheet, their arms touched and they both seemed to forget about Toni catching L.R.'s cold.

That wasn't the only thing Toni forgot (she realized later). She'd promised herself to bring up Julie's name, not the way she had last summer at the drugstore, blurting it out without any subtlety. No, this time her intention had been to drop Julie's name casually into their conversation, easily and naturally, here and there, like raisins in a muffin. Not only didn't she do it, but all afternoon with L.R. she never gave Julie a single thought.

• CHAPTER •
TWENTY-ONE

"Sweetie!" Violet put down her big green suitcase inside the door and came toward Toni with her arms out.

"Oh, Mommy," Toni said, hugging and hugging her mother, burying her face inside her mother's neck. She smelled of powder, licorice, cigarettes. Toni began patting her mother's pockets, looking for the licorice.

Then her father was there, walking slowly through the front door with a black flight bag in his hand. "Babyface." His arms were out. "There's my girl," he said with his sweet smile.

"Hello, Daddy." She slipped quickly out of his embrace, tense with her father for the first time in her life. She picked up the suitcase, slung the flight bag over her shoulder. "I'm the porter," she said in a playful voice that was too loud. She started up the stairs, wondering if they were watching her, if they were aware that something had changed. That she had changed.

Her father called plaintively after her, "Don't run away. Where are you going so fast?"

"I'll be right back," she said brightly. But in her parents' room the image came to her again of her father with a hard-knuckled fist and her mother crumpled on the floor. She dropped the flight bag, the bag with *his* things in it, as if it were a nest of snakes, and went out quickly.

Downstairs, her mother was making a pot of cocoa. She commented on the flowers, tiny white asters with rosy centers, that Toni had picked in a field and put in a jar in the middle of the table. Her mother noticed that everything was clean and in order. "You really took care of things, sweetheart."

Toni leaned against the counter. She glanced at her father, who was sitting at the table, glanced at him and then away, at him and away. There was a kind of buzzing in her head, a swaying, wavering dizziness. She looked at him. Her father. Hal. Harold . The same father she'd always known, a big man with a round face, a little too much weight on him, sweating as always, easygoing as always. And at the same time in her head was the father Martine had given her: a violent father, angry, his arm raised, his lips thin with frustration, fury.

"So how do I look to you, Babyface?" he said, leaning back in his chair. "Look in the right place." He tapped his belly, grinning at her.

"Good . . . you look good. You're thinner."

"Lost ten pounds," he said proudly.

A familiar sweetness, an ache of feeling for him, came over Toni. Her father! Her darling father. Daddy! But Martine had said . . . Could she have gotten things wrong? It was all so long ago. She might have mixed things up, exaggerated . . . or gotten confused. Toni's head began to ache.

Her father buttered a slice of bread, rolled it over, ate it, buttered another slice.

"Trying to find those lost pounds again?" her mother said.

"Oh, I've missed this butter." Her father chewed. "Baby, tell your mother she's being a food cop."

"Food cop?" Toni echoed dully.

"Right. She isn't supposed to take responsibility for what I eat. Or do. Or don't do. This is an important point. That was one very good thing at that place, the get-off-my-back sessions for spouses."

"Tell him there were a few other good things," her mother said.

"Rules for living," her father said, drawling out the words. "Toni, I tell you it was like being in the Army again. Hup two three four. No free will."

"He needs to face reality," her mother remarked to Toni.

"Tell her if reality makes you unhappy, what good is it?"

They were doing it again, talking to each other through Toni. Tell her . . . Tell him . . . Her chest felt hard and tight. Maybe she was having a heart attack. YOUNGEST VICTIM ON RECORD DIES AS "LOVING" PARENTS BICKER.

Why had she never seen that they were using her, like a pipeline or a telephone . . . or a fence. How could she have lived in such ignorance for so long? And now she blushed; ashamed, furious, thinking of the Jensens, thinking of Julie and herself. She'd always felt a little sorry for Julie, maybe even a little superior, because the Jensens were so crude, unthinking, while the Chessmores were so good, outstanding. A perfect little family unit: that was the story she'd believed. That was the story her parents had let her believe.

"Tell him you have to be motivated from within. You have to take charge of your life, and reality is part of that," her mother said.

"Tell her I know the jargon as well as she does." Her father whistled a little tune. He smiled at Toni, winking to show that this was all in fun, just part of the familiar game. They were both smiling at her, and Toni smiled back. Felt compelled to smile back, the smile of an actress playing a part she'd played for years, knew by heart.

Yes, that was it! They were all in a play; it was called *The Happy Family*, and they were all reciting lines they knew by heart. The cast was Toni, Innocent, Lovable Daughter. (She believed in the goodness and perfection of her world and never noticed that everything might not be flawless.) And Violet and Harold, Devoted Married Couple. (Oh, yes, they had their little moments of bickering, but it was only cute, they'd never had an instant of real trouble between them.)

Toni wanted to tell them they could stop acting, the play was over. They could all stop reciting their lines and start telling the truth. But she didn't know how to say it. She didn't even know how to start to say it. Her head hurt, and she went out of the kitchen.

"You forgot my good-night kiss," her father called after her.

She was halfway up the stairs. "Take a rain check, Dad."

• CHAPTER •
TWENTY-TWO

Toni and L.R. had no classes together. She looked around for him in the halls, and at lunchtime finally saw him in the gym—where else?—on the pegboard. That hadn't changed since last semester. Nor had her shyness, not enough, anyway, because she just glanced in, saw him hanging on the pegboard, and raced by.

It took her the entire weekend to work up the nerve to call him. She did it Sunday night, from her room. She knew it was his father who answered when she heard him say, "A girl for you, son." And then something else she couldn't make out, said with a laugh. And exactly as if she were there, in L.R.'s house, in that room, being teased by his father, her face flushed with heat.

"Hello?" L.R. said.

"Hi," Toni said in a too soft, embarrassed voice. She puffed out a breath. "Hello! It's Toni."

"It's you?" He sounded happy enough that her face got even hotter. "Where are you, at home?"

"Yes. In my room."

"You have your own phone? Cool."

"I got it for my birthday in May." She thought of telling him how she and Julie shared their birthdays. She'd written Julie last night but somehow hadn't mentioned bowling or L.R. Was it dishonest to leave L.R. out? She'd left out a lot of other stuff, too—everything Martine had told her.

He was saying something about a music group he liked. Toni had lost the thread. "I don't know them. I'm ignorant," she said.

"Oh, no, just uninformed," L.R. said with a laugh.

"Ignorant," she said. "Ignorance is supposed to be bliss. Is it?" She'd never actually understood what that meant until now. Yet she had been the perfect example, ignorant and blissful. She said, "L.R., do you think anyone could like being ignorant?"

"You mean, they know they're ignorant and do they like it?"

"No, no, no. They don't know but they are. They're fools in a way, they're more or less in the dark about everything. They have the wrong ideas about everything but don't know it."

"If they don't know it," he said, "it's not a fair question, is it? You can only like or not like being ignorant if you're aware of it. Then you have a choice."

"You're right," Toni said. "All right. Good-bye." She reddened at her abruptness. She hadn't meant to say that. She seemed not entirely in her own control anymore.

"Good-bye," he said. "Did you call mainly to ask me that question?"

"Yes, to ask your advice."

"Anytime," he said. "Good-bye."

She felt calm, even happy, when she hung up. She

thought about L.R. But five minutes later her mood changed. She heard her parents moving around downstairs, and she began to breathe hard. She shut her door. She put a chair against it. She wished she could make a sign. KEEP OUT! KEEP OUT! KEEP OUT!

At the supper table Toni noticed her mother's mouth moving silently, as if she were talking to herself. Had she always done that? Violet seemed tired. Her face looked shrunken, tiny. Her father, too, seemed to have shrunk. The heart attack? The lost weight? Toni studied her parents, watched them in a way she never had before. Noticed things she'd never noticed before. Noticed how often their mouths said one thing, their bodies something else.

"Milk, Hal?" her mother asked.

Her father paused, fork in midair. His lips shone with grease from the oil he'd poured on his salad. "Thanks, no." His words polite, his lips twisted to one side. "Drinking that two-percent stuff is like taking a dose of milk of magnesia."

"Sorry. I won't buy it again." Her mother's words, careful, concerned, her fingertips pushing aside the milk carton, as if even to touch it was to be unpleasantly rebuked.

"Before you ask, I skipped my walk today," her father said. "I was tired."

Toni looked down at her plate. Why did he make excuses for himself? Even if he was tired, he was supposed to walk. He didn't have to walk fast. He just had to do it. When she was a little girl, she had thought her father could be anything or do anything. He could be the president, a brilliant scientist, a great singer. She thought he was perfect, kind, brave, wonderful in every way.

Now she was appalled that he wasn't even a little bit brave. He wasn't doing the things the doctor had told him to do, the things he needed to do for his own health. He sabotaged the shopping list, came home with rich desserts, with fatty meat and snacks and treats. "For you, sweetie," he'd say to Toni. Or sometimes, "I bought this for Violet, your mom needs a little flesh on her." And then later, at the table, with a smile, it would be, "Babyface, give your dad a tiny taste of that ice cream . . . let me have one of those fries . . . I'll just take a bite of steak. . . ."

Toni looked down, couldn't bear to see her father chewing and swallowing, dizzy with shame for him, shame for herself, remembering how safe she used to feel—safe all the time, safe, happy, snug. Oblivious of everything, asleep in her palace of dreams. And now she was awake, only it wasn't a prince with a kiss who had wakened her, but her sister with a story.

The moon was hammering into Toni's eyes. She woke, went down the hall toward the bathroom. As she passed her parents' room, she heard their voices rising and falling in the darkness. She must have heard them that way hundreds of times, thousands of times, the words indistinguishable, only the whispery blur of their voices coming to her. She stood there for a moment, listening, as if she would hear something that would explain everything, that finally would answer all her questions.

Still later, she woke from a strange disturbing dream. In

the dream she was asking her mother if she and her father would get a divorce. Her mother was standing on a ladder. "Go away with your questions," she said in a silly voice. "Questions, questions, questions." Then the scene switched and Toni saw her father lying on his back on the wet green lawn. His hands were crossed over his chest. His face was red, and she thought he was dead. Her heart beat in her ears. Then he opened one eye slowly and slowly winked at her. "Gotcha!" he said, pleased with himself.

Then she woke up.

• CHAPTER • TWENTY-THREE

"Why do you live with just your father?" Toni asked L.R.

"My parents are divorced. My sister, Betsy, lives with my mother in Scranton. We switch parents for a month in the summer."

"Is it awful that they're divorced?"

L.R. shrugged. "You get used to it. It didn't work out last summer. My mom and her boyfriend drove across the country. Betsy went with them, but I stayed here. I don't like my mother's boyfriend."

"What's it like when your parents are divorced?" They were standing outside school. "Do you mind me asking all these questions?"

"No, I don't care. It's like I had a divorce, too. I'm pretty much used to it now, but sometimes I forget. I'm just walking home or something, and I think, Wait till I tell Mom this, or I think I'll see my sister and she'll be messing around my room, and I start getting mad. Then I remember I don't have to get mad. I won't even see her."

They walked slowly across the street. "My parents almost got divorced once," Toni said suddenly.

• —— •

"Toni," her mother called up the stairs. "Take the phone, Martine wants to talk to you."

"Hi, Martine," Toni said.

"I don't have a lot of time," said gracious Martine right off the bat. "I just wanted to say hello and that I miss you."

"You do not," Toni said.

"Well, I do, in a way. I admit you were a pain a lot of the time—"

"Thanks so much."

"—but you were kind of okay, too."

That was a compliment, coming from Martine.

"But let me get to the point. Do you want to come here for Christmas? Alex and I will take you out. We'll do a lot of stuff. Rockefeller Center, a play, eat out. We'll have fun. It was actually his idea."

"He sounds nice. Are you going to marry him?"

"I'll try to."

Toni laughed. "What does that mean?"

"It means I have to learn to trust myself. I have a problem with this. Every time I start getting happy, I also start thinking it can't possibly work out." Her voice faded, then came back. "It's those damn parents of ours. Don't repeat that."

"Well, I wouldn't," Toni said. "Christmas? It sounds like . . ." She hesitated, was going to say "fun." *Did* it sound like fun? What was Alex like? Opposites attract. That meant he should be cheerful, talkative, emotional. Maybe Julie could go with her. She'd be back by then, and—no, not enough room in Martine's apartment. Herself, Martine, Alex.

"Think it over," Martine said. "Let me know. I should hang up now, I've got a dinner date."

"With Alex?"

"No, three old girlfriends. Nancy, Jane, and Cynthia. We met years ago when we were all on our first jobs. We were all lowly types that everyone ordered around. Get me this! Get me that! We called ourselves the get-me girls. Now we get together and remember the bad old days."

"Are you the prettiest one?"

"What does that matter? Anyway, I'm not. Nancy is, she's gorgeous."

"She isn't as pretty as you."

"How do you know?"

"I know."

"You never even saw her, knucklehead."

Toni laughed with surprise. Insulted by her sister! Now *that* was nice.

Writing to Julie, Toni again made no mention of L.R. She could easily have thrown down a few casual words. *Julie, guess what? L.R. and I have become friends. We talk on the phone sometimes. See each other in school a little. No big deal. Jul, he's probably the nicest boy I've ever known. Remember how we used to think he was so mysterious? Well, Julie, he's actually just the opposite. He's frank and honest. He is the way he is, nothing hidden. I like that, Julie!*

Fine, but what if Julie misunderstood? What if the word *friend* escaped Julie's notice? What if Toni said too much—or too little? That decided her; she'd wait until Julie came home. It wasn't that long now. Another week, maybe two. Time had again started moving swiftly since school began.

When Julie returned, Toni and she would talk about everything, about L.R. and Julie's parents, and Toni's, too. That was something else she hadn't written about to Julie.

Later, lying in bed, petting Paws, Toni thought about L.R. for a long time, and then about Julie, and *then* about the two of them, L.R. and Julie. The two of them together. Would they hit it off immediately, the way she and L.R. had? Would Julie make him laugh? Would he sympathize with her family problems? She imagined them in a car, L.R. at the wheel. (Too young to have a license, but so what, she needed a car for the plot of this fantasy.) Okay. In the car, tooling along, Julie's hair blowing in the wind. They're on their way to a drive-in movie. Right. They're there, parked, the big screen looming ahead of them.

Julie is near the window. Aren't they too far apart? Like a puppet master, Toni gives them a shove. Hmmm. They could be closer. Another little push. Better. But why are they looking in different directions? She turns their heads toward each other. Fine. Now they have to talk.

L.R., isn't it wonderful that Toni brought us together?

Julie, what do you mean she brought us together?

Well, L.R., maybe Toni didn't tell you, but my dear best friend always had in mind that the two of us, you and I, would become best, best, best *friends.*

Julie! You don't mean that Toni was friendly with me just *to help us along?*

Oh, no, L.R. Toni liked you, she certainly did, but . . . she knew you were mine.

Yours, Julie? Is that what you said, yours?

Well, L.R., only in a manner of speaking, of course! I mean, I don't own *you, but I did see you first. Yes. And without my dear friend Toni, we would not be here in this drive-in movie together, having such a wonderful time!*

L.R. and Julie move closer. Closer still. Is a kiss coming?

Wait, Toni calls, *maybe you guys want to think about this!* L.R. and Julie don't seem to hear her. Well, how can they? They are in the car, she is out here. Suddenly she's in the car, too. Although they don't know it. She's in the backseat, right behind them. And just in time, just as their smiles are about to merge, she pops up and thrusts her head between them. *Oh, Toni,* they both say. *Toni! Here you are.* And they smile at her. And forget all about kissing.

• CHAPTER •
TWENTY-FOUR

In the morning when she went downstairs to make breakfast, Toni saw her father outside in the yard, smoking. He heard her and turned quickly, guiltily. "Just needed to smell it," he said, and heeled out the cigarette. But gradually, over the next few days, he took up smoking again. Although, as he said, it was only four or five a day now, not like his old two-pack-a-day habit. "I'm feeling nervous about things," he said. "A cigarette helps. It calms me." He had gone back to work, half time, but there was a question about his ability to remain on the truck. He might have to apply for a desk job.

They were all in the family room eating popcorn, watching TV. Her mother was lying on the couch. Her father was in one chair, Toni in another. "You shouldn't be smoking," her mother said.

Toni's eyes swiveled to her mother, then her father.

"I don't smoke in the house," her father said.

"That's not what I meant. You shouldn't be smoking."

"One or two a day isn't going to hurt me. Moderation."

Her mother put her hands behind her head. Her eyes switched to Toni. "Have you done your homework, sweetheart?"

A perfectly normal question. A perfectly normal moment. Her father had turned toward Toni, too. They were both looking at her, as they often did, with their special we-love-you-and-adore-you smiles. And suddenly, with a kind of mental grinding of gears, Toni's vision shifted, and she saw, not her familiar parents but two enormous puppets. Puffed-up faces, large, boxy bodies, mouths slashed red, hands like mitts, voices creaking out from behind the masks of their faces. "HAVE YOU DONE YOUR HOMEWORK, SWEETHEART?" the giant puppet mother said. "WHERE ARE YOU GOING, BABYFACE?" the giant puppet father said.

Panicked, Toni ran. She ran to her room, fell on the bed and pulled the pillow over her head. Was she going crazy? She felt dizzy with emotions; they came at her in great sweeps of feeling like fat, hard clouds blowing through her. She cried. She cried harder, hiding her head under the pillow. *Don't hear me—don't come up the stairs . . . don't come in here . . . leave me alone.* She sat up. Her eyes ached, her head felt hollow and bony. She remembered, as if from a long time ago, that she used to enjoy crying, that there had been something satisfying, pleasurable, in letting go, crying ceaselessly, fast and soft. Afterward she would feel limp, peaceful, a calm lake after a storm. But these tears were different; these were hard tears, tears like stones.

Walking into the house after school, Toni put down her books. "Paws?" she called, but it was her father who appeared, coming through the door from the kitchen.

He brushed his hand back and forth in the air. "Good day in school, Babyface?" His eyes were red-rimmed.

"Mom is going to smell the smoke," Toni said.

"I'll open a window." He gave her a complicitous smile. "Her sniffer isn't as sharp as yours."

"That's what you think," Toni said.

"We'll see, we'll see." He was playful, like a boy throwing a ball, ignoring that no one wanted to catch it. "Want to take a bet on that?" He laid his hand on her head, frowzed up her hair.

A heavy heat filled Toni's chest. She wanted to shove her father's hot, heavy hand off her head. *Grow up! Stop smoking. I don't want to play your little games. And don't call me Babyface. I'm not your Babyface. I refuse.*

Did he "hear" her? Did the words, like little poison darts, fly from her mind to his? Bending a little, looking at her, his face went soft and red, wondering. "Are you okay, sweetheart?" he said. "Are you hungry? I'm making a bread pudding—eggs, milk, a little cream, cinammon—it's going to be good."

Eggs, milk, cream. More things he wasn't supposed to have. She remembered Julie once saying, "Your father is like Humpty Dumpty, he's round and soft and loves to feed people." Toni had laughed. "What's Humpty Dumpty got to do with feeding people?" And Julie had said, "I don't know, he was an egg, wasn't he? Food, himself."

Now the image stayed in Toni's mind. Her father as Humpty Dumpty, the round white egg teetering on the wall. If he fell, he would have a great, great fall.

• CHAPTER •
TWENTY-FIVE

"A friend of mine says one of his uncles had the same thing you do, Mom." Toni put down a tray with food on the table next to her mother's bed. "And a chiropractor helped him a lot."

"I don't believe in them," her mother said.

She had thrown out her back. "Ridiculous," she kept saying. "Ridiculous the way it happened. I wasn't doing anything!" She had, in fact, opened a bureau drawer to take out a scarf when, in a moment, she found herself on the floor, in pain and unable to move. She had lain there, helpless as a bug on its back, for over an hour, until Toni found her. The doctor had put Violet in traction for five days. After that she was to stay in bed for at least a week.

"L.R.'s uncle didn't stay in bed more than a couple of days."

"Where's your father?" her mother said.

"Maybe you just want to *try* the chiropractor?" Toni said.

"No, I don't."

"Why not? You keep complaining about missing work."

"I just don't want to, Toni. Is your father coming in to eat?"

Toni went to the window. Why was her mother so stubborn? Would it hurt to try something different? "Dad," she called. She rapped on the glass. He was in the backyard, raking. "Do you want to eat with Mom?"

Toni and her father had moved the TV from the family room into the bedroom for her mother, and they watched while they ate. Toni only half looked or listened. It was the evening news, something about a country called Mozambique in Africa. Starving children. She turned away. It was too sad. Why should people be hungry? Then, right afterward, came happy singing ads for shampoo and cars. Then the news again. Child abuse this time. A man being led away, his head bowed.

"People like that shouldn't have kids," her father said.

And Toni said, "Why did you hit Mom?"

She hadn't known she was going to say it.

Her father stared at her. There were little broken red veins on his nose. One of them flared like a red flower. His eyes switched to the TV. Then he glanced at her. And again his eyes went to the TV.

"What did you say?" It was her mother who spoke first. "Hit? What are you talking about? Where did you get such an idea? Who told you that?" her mother said.

Toni looked at her father. "How could you do that? How could you? I thought I knew you. Who are you?" The words came out of her, breathless, sucked out of her.

"Who told you?" her mother asked again. "Who told you all this stuff? Martine? She shouldn't have done that!"

Toni crumpled her napkin. Why didn't her father speak? How could he just sit there like a frog on a log? A fat frog on a log! "I always thought you were so perfect." Her voice shook.

"It has nothing to do with you," her mother said. "It was before you were born. Nothing to do with you," she repeated. And finally her father moved; he thrust aside the little tray table and stood up. "Hal," her mother said. "Don't get yourself upset." He gave her a single blank and furious look and walked out.

"You upset him." Her mother hit the control on the TV. The picture went off with a little thump of light. "Toni, you know he's not well, how could you do that to him?"

Toni looked down at the food on her plate, repulsive lumps of brown meat. "How could you just go back to living with him, as if nothing happened?"

"How could I? I'll tell you how." Her mother's little pale face flamed up. "I could because of you. You were more important, that's how."

"You were going to split. Martine told me. He was gone already."

"So what?" her mother said. "I don't understand what you're saying. What is the point? Why drag this up now?"

"You kept me ignorant. I had a whole different idea of our family, of him." Toni's throat swelled. She felt awful. She didn't know why she had started this. "You never told me anything."

"Of course I didn't tell you! Why would I? It wasn't a happy time. What matters is that you were born, and I loved you, we both loved you. We made up our differences, we put aside our differences for you."

"I always thought you were so happy. I thought you loved each other."

"Who are you to say we don't?"

Toni stared at her mother. "What did you get out of it?"

"A life," her mother said. "My life. Let me tell you something, Toni, you don't know that much about love. It's not from a storybook. There are different kinds of love. Your father and I have been through a lot together." She was speaking fast. "Thirty years together. Don't you think that counts for something? Thirty years we've stuck it out. What we did, we did for you. We have you. We've always had that."

"Stuck it out?" Toni repeated, horrified.

Her mother sliced her hand through the air. "Don't get into words with me. Maybe I didn't say it right. We stuck—stayed together. Is that a crime? What was the alternative? Would you have wanted to grow up without your father? Or not be here at all?"

Toni didn't answer. She held her throat. She was the glue that had kept them together? It made her feel sick. Her parents' lives were awful. Everything she had thought true was untrue. Everything she had thought real was unreal.

Pretense and sacrifice—that was her parents' lives. Pretending to be happy, happy together, a happy family. And they had done it for her! She squeezed her hands together. Why? Why would anybody choose unhappiness? Choose to make somebody else responsible for their unhappiness? Was this the way she would live when she grew up?

She took the tray with the dishes downstairs. Her father was lying on the couch in the living room. "Toni!" She stood in the doorway, looking at him. The back of his hand was over his eyes. "Why are you doing this to me, Toni?" he said. "You think I'm the only man in the world who ever lost it and hit someone?"

"It wasn't *someone.* It was Mom. It was my mother."

"And I'm your father," he said, his hand still over his eyes. "I put you here on this earth, and I'm going to tell you something, and I want you to listen. I'm telling you that it was something awful in my life. You weren't involved. It's not your business. So do you think you can forget this? It happened once. Only once. Once," he repeated. "And there's such a thing as being human. Making mistakes."

Words. Words, words. She lost the meaning of them. She heard them as sounds in her head. Words. Just words.

"It shouldn't have happened," he said. "You think I don't know that? You think I wasn't sorry?"

As if from a distance, she gazed at him as he lay on the couch, his hand limp over his eyes, telling her to forget the awful thing he had done. She seemed to see him as if for the first time. Forget? Why? She felt tough, unyielding. She would never forget what he'd done. He wasn't the person she'd believed he was. No, he wasn't! A hot breath swept through her. She felt betrayed. Forget? No. Never. Even though it had happened before she was born, she would never forget.

• CHAPTER •
TWENTY-SIX

Kelly Lutz sat down next to Toni in the cafeteria and opened a carton of milk. Last week her hair had been short, straight, and pink. Today her head was shaved with only a tuft of bright red curls left on top. "So, do you like it?" she asked.

"Don't you get tired of changing it?" Toni said.

"Noooo! Tell the truth now."

"It's cute. It shows off your eyes."

"Leon Victor did it. I'll have to tell him you like it. He always cuts his sister's hair. He came over the other day. I got the scissors and said, 'Leon. Cut.' "

"How did you know he could do a good job?"

"I didn't." Kelly laughed raucously. "But I'm a person with faith. You should have heard my mother scream when she saw it. I said, 'Ma, this isn't even a new style anymore. Lisa Bonet had her hair cut like this a trillion years ago.' You know what my mother said? 'Who's Lisa Bonet?' Uh-oh!" she elbowed Toni. "Your throb just walked in."

Toni followed Kelly's eyes. L.R. was standing in the doorway of the cafeteria. "He's just a friend."

"Uhhh-huh," Kelly drawled disbelievingly. "So how come I keep seeing you two together?"

"I told you, we're just friends."

"Riiiight. And now ask me if I think a boy and a girl can be *just friends*. Sure they can, in pig heaven."

L.R. was approaching. Toni noted that he'd just had his hair cut, too. So did Kelly. "L.R., where'd you get your hair cut?" she said.

"Design Line."

"How much did you pay? You should go to my guy. He's free." Kelly gave her loud laugh.

L.R. looked at Toni. "Want to go outside until the bell?"

"Who, me?" Kelly winked at him.

Toni stood, crumpling her paper bag.

"Bye-bye, kiddies. Have fun." This time Kelly winked at Toni.

A noise woke Toni in the middle of the night. She sat up and listened. At the foot of the bed, Paws made dream sounds. But that wasn't what had awakened Toni. She heard it again, a rattling at the window. She got out of bed. The moon was up, and she could see someone under the plum tree, a dark shape, a lifted arm.

She ran down the stairs, through the kitchen, out the back door. Julie emerged from under the tree. "It's about time you woke up," she said. "I was getting tired of throwing gravel."

"Did you just get here?" The grass was cool under Toni's bare feet.

"About twenty minutes ago."

They stood there, looking at each other, and neither one moved. It was so strange, awkward. "So here I am," Julie said.

"Here you are," Toni said. She was aware of Julie's flat, ironic voice, aware of herself standing motionless. She had thought of this moment so often, had imagined screaming, shouting with joy. Calling Julie's name. Had imagined them both jumping around, excited, tearful.

"Julie," she said. "Wow, I can't quite believe it."

"Me, either."

Toni smiled. "So am I awake?"

"You're not dreaming," Julie said.

"Wow," Toni said again; and then, at the same moment, they moved toward each other, hugged, and did a little dance in place on the wet grass.

• CHAPTER •
TWENTY-SEVEN

In Julie's room, they lay around on the beds, chewing pistachios and tossing the shells into the wastebasket. "I keep expecting Heather to walk in and order me off her bed," Toni said with a little laugh.

Julie thumped her feet restlessly. "Believe it or not, I miss that brat. This house seems so empty." Heather had decided to stay on in San Francisco with her aunt Wendy.

"Was your mother upset about leaving her there?"

"Jerrine? Lord knows what goes on with Jerrine. I can't pull that woman apart."

Had Julie always talked that way, used those expressions? *Lord knows . . . can't pull that woman apart . . .* Had she always been so restless? She couldn't seem to stay still for a moment.

She got up and started brushing her hair. "Want to fetch a guess why Jerrine decided to come back?"

"Fetch a what?"

"Oh, that's my aunt. Wendy says these weird things. When my mother heard that my father had left Alaska and was on his way east, she suddenly couldn't bear the way we were living *one more moment.* She was Mrs. Whirlwind, she was ordering everyone around. Do this, do that, we're gonna go! Now my father is in Buffalo, and Jerrine thinks it's just a quick stop on his way home."

Julie sat down and studied her face in the mirror. "Do I look worn-out? Haggard? Old? I'm serious. Look at these dark circles under my eyes." Toni went to Julie and hugged her. Julie leaned against her. "Look at that puffy stuff, aren't those bags under my eyes? My mother says everything shows on your face in time."

"Your eyes look fine, maybe a little tired."

Julie opened a jar and began brushing color rapidly on her cheeks. "Toni, am I going to be incredibly far behind in school?"

"Why? They must do the same stuff in San Francisco as we do here."

"Who knows?" Julie swiveled around. "Toni, I was dumb, I didn't do anything there. I didn't want to do anything. I was failing."

"You, failing?"

Tears came up in Julie's eyes. "It was stupid of me, but it was the way I felt. Now I'll be behind everyone."

"You'll catch up. I'll help you, I'm sure it'll be okay."

"You're always sure things will be okay," Julie said. She pushed her chair back. "Did I tell you my mother bought a car out there and then had to sell it for practically nothing? We even borrowed money from Wendy to come home. She doesn't have anything, either!"

"You know, we've been talking about your stuff for three days," Toni remarked.

"Meaning what?"

"Meaning I have stuff, too."

"Fine. We'll talk about your stuff. Just don't tell me about your father's heart attack. I don't need to be more depressed."

With that, Toni put off again telling Julie about Martine and her parents. But there was one subject she had to bring up, and the sooner the better. "Will hearing about L.R. depress you?"

"L.R.? I don't see why it should. Is he still wearing black T-shirts and dark glasses?"

Toni nodded. "Exactly. I have some information you might like knowing. Why he wears the dark glasses and what his initials stand for."

"Okay."

"Dark glasses because his eyes are light-sensitive."

"Medical reason? How disillusioning."

"And L.R. stands for . . . want to guess?"

"Larry Richard."

"Try again."

"Lewis Robert . . . Lefty Ricky . . . Laurence Rider . . . Tell. I don't know."

"Little Rose."

"Little *Rose?*"

"It's the family name for the first son. He's the fourth generation in his family to have that name. His father is Big Rose, and L.R. is Little Rose. Get it? Little Rose. L.R."

"How do you know all this?"

"I asked him."

Julie gazed intently at her. "You asked him? You asked Little Rose?"

"Julie, don't ever call him that to his face," Toni warned. "He doesn't go around telling people his real name."

"Why not? I think it's kind of adorable. Little Rose. I love it! Little Rose, Little Rose, Little Rose." She sprang up and stood over Toni. "Why did Little Rose tell you his name?"

"I told you . . . I asked him." Toni told herself she didn't have to feel guilty for becoming L.R.'s friend.

"You asked him? You? My shy, embarrassed friend?"

"Julie—"

"Wow! This is pretty incredible. You go up to somebody you've never talked to before, and . . . what did you say to him? 'I've never talked to you before, but tell me what your initials stand for!'?"

"No, Jul, it wasn't like that." Toni laughed, but she felt uncomfortable.

"Well, what was it like?"

Toni wished Julie would move a little, give her some space. She swung her legs over the side of the bed. Here it was, the moment to tell how she had met L.R. in the office and how one thing had led to another. Should she start with that first day? Or skip that and go to the phone call? But without Mrs. Evelyn and L.R.'s lost key and their lockers being so close, would the phone call make sense?

"It wasn't in school that I asked him about his name. Do you remember that I talked to him last summer in the drugstore?"

"Sure, I remember. That was nothing. You wrote me about it. It was, Hi, hello, good-bye. You didn't ask him about his name."

"Right. But I've gotten to know him pretty well since school started."

"You're in a class together," Julie decided.

"No, not that. Our lockers are near each other. We've been talking and . . . you know. He's very understanding."

"For a boy," Julie said.

"For anyone."

"More understanding than me?"

"Not fair, Julie. It's different."

"What do you talk about?"

"Nothing special. School, our parents—stuff. His mom and dad are divorced. He lives with his father, his sister lives with his mother." Toni studied Julie's face. "We went bowling, Julie. That's when he told me about his name."

"Bowling? Are you making this up? I mean, this is pretty wild. My shy girlfriend bowling with the cutest boy in school!"

Toni smiled, she couldn't help it. "He taught me to keep score," she blurted.

"And what else did he teach you?"

"Julie, don't take it like that. You have to meet him. He's much better in person than from afar."

"I'm delighted to hear it." She looked at Toni closely. "You're wearing makeup. When did that start?"

"Only a little eye shadow. Does it look okay?"

"What's going on, Toni? I couldn't wait to get back home. That's all I thought about for months, being in my own house again, being with you, everything the way it was before. And now I'm here and nothing's the same. My sister's in San Francisco, my father's still crapping around somewhere, I'm going to be behind everyone in school, and even you aren't the same. Even you! You've changed, you're different. Damn it, Toni, you're just not the same!" Julie's lips quivered.

What did Julie want her to say? Toni could make a speech, too. *So what if I'm not the same? Why should I be? Sure, I've changed. I wouldn't want to be the same person you left behind! That was three months ago, Julie, a long time. Time enough for anyone to change.* "Things happened to me, too, Julie."

"Your father's heart attack? At least—"

"That, and more than that." Toni cut Julie off before she could start with the at-least-your-parents-love-each-other stuff.

"You would never have cheated behind my back before," Julie said.

Toni was stung. "If you mean L.R., Julie, let me tell you that I made friends with him for you."

"Oh, come on!" Julie pushed her hair off her face. "For me? The way my mother went back and forth across the country for me?"

"I *w-was* thinking of you," Toni stammered.

Julie ran her hand over Toni's head. "Where's your halo? I don't see your halo."

"I always had in mind for you to get together with him. The two of you."

Julie bent over—was she laughing? was she crying?—and came up with her face scrunched hotly. "Tell the truth. You're the one who's always going on about honesty. So be honest, Toni! You just had the hots for him."

"Jul!"

"What have you two done, Toni? How far have you gone?"

Toni could have saved it at that moment—possibly—if she'd laughed. She didn't. She got stiff-necked and self-righteous, maybe because she was feeling guilty about L.R. and thinking that Julie was at least half right. "If you're going to be like that, Jul, I don't want to talk about it."

"That far, huh?" Julie drawled.

Then Toni lost it entirely. "What kind of stupid remark is that? You're not in a movie yet, Julie!"

"Oh, don't be so smart." Julie slammed her hairbrush down on the dressing table. They were shouting at each other. "I suppose you're going to tell me you and L.R. are none of my business?"

"That's right! Thank you for saying it." Toni couldn't believe that she and Julie were fighting over a boy. Or were they fighting over something else? More than L.R.?

"So what are you staring at with your mouth open?" Julie said. "Go away. Go home. Go. Go!"

• CHAPTER •
TWENTY-EIGHT

In the gym, nibbling on a sandwich, Toni leaned against the door, watching L.R. working out on the mats. When he finished, she thought how much she liked the way he looked, sweating, smiling, catching his breath. He bought a can of juice from the vending machine near the door and they went outside.

It was a warm day and everyone was out. Toni and L.R. sat down on the grass under the flagpole. She was telling him about chorale tryouts when she saw Julie coming down the steps. She was wearing wide pajama pants and a shirt printed with splashy purple flowers, short enough to show a strip of belly and back. Very California.

Toni touched the friendship bracelet she was wearing, identical to one Julie had, a narrow band of green and black plastic strands woven together in a diamond pattern. Here it was Tuesday and they hadn't made up their fight, hadn't even tried. She leaned forward, her lips tunneling to form Julie's name. Julie glanced up, then passed by. The flowers on her shirt seemed to wink coolly at Toni.

"Do you want me to come to the chorale tryouts with you?" L.R. asked. "Sort of be backup for you?"

Julie had stopped to light a cigarette. She said something to Kelly Lutz and Leon Victor, and they all began laughing. Their three heads—Kelly's purple, Leon's black, Julie's honey—shone and bent together in the thin October sunlight.

"Or would my being there make you nervous?" L.R. asked.

"I doubt anything can make me more nervous than I already am," she said. Was it possible she would be trying out for chorale at last, but without Julie there?

She remembered the summer she and Julie were eight and had done nothing but make friendship bracelets for hours on end. And another summer she had spent trying to teach Julie all the songs she knew. And the grief she had felt just months ago when she knew Julie was going to California.

Julie, Leon, and Kelly were still laughing theatrically, throwing up their arms as if they could hardly contain their merriment. What could Julie, the melancholy Julie, have said to set them all off like that?

Fiddling with the friendship bracelet, Toni had worked it off her wrist. She held it out to L.R.

"What?" he said.

"For you. A present."

Momentarily he looked doubtful. Boys in their school wore earrings and necklaces, not bracelets. Then he took it, pushed it over his hand. It had been tight on her wrist, it was tighter on his. "I should give you something else," she said.

L.R. took off the bracelet and put it in his pocket. "I'm happy with this. . . . Now I have to give you something."

"No you don't . . . what?"

"I don't know. I'll think of something. Some friendly something." He was looking at her and smiling. She saw herself in his dark glasses.

Toni took down the rake and a shovel and opened the garage door. It was a perfect fall day, cool, the sky blue, unclouded. Across the way, she saw Julie clipping a rosebush. Toni banged down the garage door and Julie glanced up. For a moment they stared at each other. She and Julie were still avoiding each other. They didn't speak, they didn't walk to school together, they passed each other in the halls looking the other way. It was too strange.

Toni held up the shovel. "Want to go to a funeral?"

"Who's dead?" Julie drawled. "Paws?"

You asked for it, Toni told herself, but still, what a mean thing to say! No, no one was dead, but maybe some*thing* was—their friendship. In the past Toni had almost always been the one to make up first. Right now, right this moment, if she walked across the lawn and said, "Julie, I'm sorry, it was my fault," wouldn't that do it? Wouldn't it be all over with? "Julie, of course I should have told you about L.R. sooner! And I shouldn't have gone bowling with him! Of course not!" Toni could imagine the dialogue, but she couldn't get any *feeling* into it. She wasn't sorry about L.R. How could she be! And she *had* been sincere about wanting him and Julie to like each other. So, no, this time she didn't feel like being the first to apologize. And no, she didn't feel like playing good Toni for one more moment.

She went around the side of the house and began raking the leaves and twigs shed by the big willow tree. It was an autumn chore that her father had always done before. She raked the stuff into a pile down at the bottom of the yard, then shoveled dirt over it. When she looked up, she saw Julie coming toward her, hands in the back pockets of her pants. She stopped on the line between the two properties and stood there, watching Toni work. Toni raked ferociously. Julie chewed on a cigarette and stared. It was unnerving.

Toni dumped another shovelful of dirt on the pile of leaves. "What do you want?" she said to Julie. "If you didn't come to apologize, why don't you just leave?"

"Apologize?" Julie picked something off her lip. "You've got a nerve. Why should I apologize to you? I think it should be the reverse!"

"You know what your trouble is, Julie? You can't stand that I did something independent, that I made a friend all by myself. It makes you crazy." She cleaned leaves off the rake. "I've changed, Julie, only not the way you accused me of. I've matured, I've had things happen, things to think about—"

"What does that mean?" Julie interrupted. "You think you're different because you had to put up with your sister for a week? Or because you walked around the big city for a few days? You think that made you so mature? Oh, wait, wait, I forgot! Getting so *friendly* with L.R., that must be what matured you." She dropped the cigarette and walked away.

"Great exit," Toni called after her.

"Nice night," Toni's father said, braking at the corner. He was driving her to the mall, where she was going to do some shopping for her mother. "So how are things with you, Babyface?"

"Fine."

"You seem very quiet lately."

She shrugged.

"Is anything the matter? School okay?"

"Fine."

"What's doing there?" He pulled into the parking lot.

"Not much."

"Something must be happening," he said.

Another shrug. "I tried out for chorale today."

"I know you got in," he said. "They want your voice!"

"Maybe." The results wouldn't be posted until next week. It had been good having L.R. there. Toni had focused on him when she sang for Mrs. Sokolow, and it had helped control her nervousness.

"What's with Julie?" her father said. "I haven't seen her around much. Everything all right with you two?"

"Mmm," Toni said neutrally.

Her father pushed in the cigarette lighter. "So what am I going to do to cheer you up, tell you a joke?"

Toni shook her head quickly and reached for her purse.

Her father lit up. "I'm down to five a day," he said, as if he wanted congratulations.

She put her hand on the door handle. "You're not supposed to smoke at all."

"Babyface, I'm trying."

"You could try harder."

He smiled slightly. "We aren't all as disciplined as you. Nicotine is a powerful habit, not easy to break. . . . You want me to stop? You want to see me go cold turkey?"

"It's up to you." She opened the door, then sat there, holding the handle. "Don't call me that," she said.

"What? Don't call you what?"

"Babyface. I told you before, Dad. I'm asking you, will you stop calling me that?" Her lungs felt pinched, as if she'd inhaled a poisonous draft of his smoke.

His smile faded. "Fine. That's the way you want it—sure thing. But let me tell you something, you've got a chip on your shoulder, Daughter, and that's no way to go around in the world."

"I don't—" she began.

"You're mad at me, don't think I don't know it," he went on. "I notice you don't talk to me anymore. I notice you avoid me. I notice these things. I'm not insensitive to them. And don't think I don't know what it's all about, something that happened before you were born."

"It's not just that," she said.

"No? What is it then?" He had never spoken to her like this before, his lips thin with demand, challenging her.

She stared at him, swallowing back a rawness in her throat, and he stared at her, a flat, unfatherly look, as if they were unrelated, just two people who had found themselves unhappily together in this car.

"It's my whole life," she said. She thought of him hitting her mother, and, as always, with the thought something inside her slid away, a cold sliding as of ice down a slope. "It's—everything," she said, trying to grasp it herself. "It's all connected, everything I thought about you, everything you said to me, every way you ever acted toward me—" Her voice cracked. "It's all ruined, horrible now."

"That's in your mind," he said. "What did I ever do that wasn't out of love? I loved you, I stayed, I took care of you, I did the right thing." He stared at her intently. "You had the best of me," he said. "And this is what I get in return?"

She didn't know the words to tell him how much it hurt that she'd never known who he really was. What had he said? *That's in your mind.* Yes. The father she'd adored had been all in her mind, and like one of those balloons on a cardboard base, when a pin had been stuck in it, the air leaked out, and all that was left was a deflated rubber skin. And a bit of cardboard.

"I never lied to you," he said. "I put the past behind me. But if you can't see it, if this is the way you want it . . . Just remember that it's your choice."

She hated the way he was speaking in that hard, dismissive voice. And she hated her knowledge. And she hated that her throat was raw with anger and tears. And she hated that such awful things were happening to her with all the people she loved.

"Well," she said finally, "I better get going." She got out. The moon was rising over the back of the mall, a red harvest moon. It was beautiful, and she almost turned, almost said, "Dad, look!" But she walked away.

• CHAPTER • TWENTY-NINE

From her bedroom window Toni saw the lights go on in Julie's room across the way. Then she saw Julie pass the window, pass out of sight. "Hey, Jul," she sang out softly, "come on over, come on over." Julie passed the window again, oblivious. No magic. No ESP. No secret pull of Toni's voice or spirit. Was the little world of Toni and Julie gone then, completely and forever? For a moment, with such intensity that she almost cried, Toni wanted it, wanted that little world back.

Then she closed the window, pulled down the shade, and went to her desk, unaware of what she was going to do until she took up the scissors.

In front of the mirror she picked up a strand of hair and cut. A dark, floating spiral fell to the floor. She picked up another strand of hair. When she finally put down the scissors, her long hair was gone.

What was left had sprung into tight curls close to her head, and beneath them was her face, no longer tiny. Her tiny face was gone and in its place was a larger face, these bigger eyes, this somber face. She tried out a smile.

• —— •

"Toni, hello."

"Hello."

"How are you? Are you busy right now?"

"No. Who is this?"

"You don't know who this is?"

"Oh, sorry, is it—Mrs. Frankowitz?"

"No, this is not Mrs. Frankowitz. Try again."

"I don't think this is Mrs. Abish."

"No, it's not."

"Who is this? Heather? It's not you, is it?"

"Toni, let me put you out of your misery. This is Martine. Your sister. Martine Chessmore. Remember me?"

"Martine! Oh, I'm embarrassed. I didn't recognize your voice. I'm so embarrassed."

"Take it easy, don't be so embarrassed. It's not such a big deal."

"You sound different. Why do you sound so different? I always recognize people's voices."

"I've had laryngitis for three days. This is the first day I can talk above a whisper."

"Oh. That makes me feel better! Are you laughing at me?"

"Just a little. Anyway, I called to find out what you decided about Christmas."

"Christmas?"

"Toni, what's going on here? Christmas. Remember Christmas? Santa Claus. Jolly old St. Nick. Jingle Bells."

"Martine—"

"Christmas in New York with your sister and Alex. Remember now?"

"Martine, okay, okay, I remember!"

"And don't tell me you're embarrassed."

"I am."

"Tough. So what's the scoop? Are you coming?"

"Yes."

"Great."

"Really? You think it's great?"

"Sure. We're going to have fun. Bring your ice skates. We'll go skating at Rockefeller Center. So, anything else? Or do you want to put Mom on?"

"Mom's not here. Dad is. You want to talk to him?"

"Uhh . . . okay. Yeah. That's a good idea. Let me say hello to Dad."

"I'll get him in a minute. I want to ask you something. If someone you love has done something you think is really bad, but it wasn't done to you, but it still hurts because it makes you see that person as completely different than you ever thought he was, what do you do?"

"Toni?"

"Yes?"

"Run that by me again. If someone you love has done something wrong but not to you—"

"Right. But it really made you see that person in a whole different way, and it made you not love them in the same way—"

"Toni."

"What?"

"Are you talking about Dad?"

"Yes."

"I thought so."

"Well, what's your answer, Martine?"

"I'm thinking."

"Maybe you don't want me to ask you."

"No, it's okay. I just want to think about it. It's a good question. Did I tell you I've been going to therapy?"

"No! Why?"

"Don't panic, it doesn't mean I'm crazy or going over the edge. It just means I realized I needed some help in sorting things out. After your visit, it hit me."

"Oh, it's because of me?"

"Well, you were the catalyst. I was probably coming around to it, but I kind of scared myself that night we talked. It was so intense." Her voice faded for a moment, then came back stronger. "Anyway, it gives me someone to talk to about my feelings, someone trained and smart about these things."

"Like a guidance counselor," Toni said.

"Yeah. Except a lot more expensive. Well, about Dad—what I'm learning is that the first thing you need to do in almost any situation is to recognize your feelings."

"I do, Martine! I recognize them. That's the problem. I feel my feelings so much, and I don't know what to do with them."

"I think you have to forgive him, Toni. That's what I'm finding out that I have to do. Does it seem hard to you?"

"Yes."

"But people are more than one thing, aren't they? More than one way, not all good or all bad."

"I suppose so."

"No, come on. You don't suppose so. You know that.

Or you don't know anything."

"Hal!" Mrs. Jensen wheeled her shopping cart down the aisle toward Toni and her father. "Hal!" she said again, putting her hand on his arm. Julie was with her. The two girls glanced at each other.

"I've been meaning to come over and see you," Mrs. Jensen said. "I talked to Violet. I heard about your troubles this summer, and now Violet, her back. What a shame. Tell me, how are you doing, how are you feeling?"

"I'm hanging in there, Jerrine. What about yourself?"

"Oh . . . you know. I'm hanging in there, too."

Toni held on to the bar of the grocery cart with a distant smile. She was aware of Julie watching her.

"What else can you do?" Toni's father said in his best brave voice. "You have to make the best of things."

"Exactly! Just keep up a cheerful face, no matter what."

With a snort Julie clapped her hand over her mouth and rolled her eyes wildly. That did it. Toni was going to laugh out loud in a moment. "I'll get the cat food," she squeaked, pushing the cart away fast.

Julie went around the aisle with her. "Just keep up a cheerful face," she said in her mother's voice.

"What else can you do?" Toni said in her father's brave voice.

"Good for you, Hal!"

"Good for you, Jerrine!"

They glanced at each other slyly, from the corners of their eyes.

"I like your hair," Julie said.

Toni's hand went to her head. "Thanks."

"Yeah, it's nice. When'd you do it?"

"The other night. I just took the scissors and—" Toni made cutting motions all around her head.

"Cool," Julie said.

That was how they finally made up.

• CHAPTER •
THIRTY

Toni invited Julie and L.R. for supper Friday night when both her parents would be out, but she didn't tell either Julie or L.R. that the other was coming. Not exactly a plot, more of a ploy. Or a plan. Anyway, she just wanted to bring the two of them together. She wanted them to be friends and, if it was in the cards, more. Which would not make her feel so great, but she felt she owed it to Julie and to herself, too, to have everything clear between them.

L.R. arrived first. He was wearing baggy gray pants and the usual black T-shirt. "You're right on time," Toni said. She felt a little awkward, unsure. It was the first time L.R. had come to her house. Maybe he felt the same way. He thrust a silver freezer bag at her. "Dessert."

"Oh. Thank you."

"Ice cream cake."

"Great." She led him into the living room. "Sit down, make yourself at home."

"Thank you." He pulled at his pants legs and sat down. "Very nice house."

"Thank you," she heard herself saying again. Was that the fourth or the fifth time?

Paws came into the room and leaped onto L.R. He circled, then put his paws up against L.R.'s chest. "Hey, kitty, hey, puss, how you doing?"

"You must be a cat person," Toni said, sitting down next to him.

"We have two, Spike and Jones."

"You never told me that."

"No? My father and I both like cats." He rubbed the side of Paws's mouth. "Cats like this a lot. I read that they have special glands there. Jones goes crazy when I do it to her."

"I can hear that Paws likes it," Toni said, and she began scratching him under the neck. The cat's eyes closed in ecstasy.

In a few minutes she went into the kitchen to put the ice cream cake away and get the pizza into the oven. She was fixing the tray with soda glasses and plates when Julie opened the back door. "Supper ready?" Julie said. She was wearing a black derby hat, a shirt, and a pair of old jeans with holes in the knees.

"I thought you were going to throw out those jeans," Toni said. Maybe she should have told Julie that L.R. was going to be here. She wasn't even wearing earrings.

"I decided to use them for trashing around."

"Thanks a lot. Why don't you go put on something nicer?"

"Who am I impressing, the pizza?"

"Not exactly. You'll see." Toni took Julie's arm and

steered her into the living room. She heard Julie's little intake of breath.

L.R. stood up. "Hi."

"Oh . . . hi," Julie said.

"This is great," Toni said. "My two friends, meeting at last."

L.R. picked up Paws and pressed him to his chest. Julie stared past L.R. at the TV, as if it were an object of powerful fascination. Talk, *talk!* Toni thought. "L.R. is a really good bowler, Julie," she offered.

"Truly?" Julie murmured theatrically. "I always thought bowling was one of the lesser sports."

"Julie's an actress, L.R.," Toni said quickly. "You probably remember seeing her in June in the Drama Club play."

"Umm, sure," he said.

"She was wonderful," Toni said.

Julie wandered over to the window.

L.R. sat down, still cuddling Paws.

"Well, you guys, carry on!" Toni escaped to the kitchen.

She checked the pizza and finished preparing the tray, all the time listening for the sound of their voices. She dawdled, giving them as much time as possible.

When she came into into the living room, L.R. was lying across the couch playing with Paws. Julie was on the other side of the room, flipping dials on the TV. They weren't talking. They weren't looking at each other. The only thing they were doing mutually was ignoring each other.

"Who's ready for pizza?" Toni said. They both looked up, almost leaped up. She had never seen two more obviously relieved people. "Oh, there you are!" L.R. said.

And Julie, as if Toni had been away on a world tour, sighed, "Back at last. It's about time."

So much for plans, plots, and ploys.

• CHAPTER •
THIRTY-ONE

"Toni. I don't want to go on like this," her father said. He sat down at the kitchen table across from her. "What are we going to do about us?"

She put her finger in her book to mark her place.

Her father gestured around the kitchen. "You and me living this way, hardly talking, it's not right. When you do talk to me, it's like I'm someone from Mars." He leaned toward her. "I want my daughter back."

Her mother appeared in the doorway. "You two are talking," she said. "Good. Are you telling her some of the things we've been discussing, Hal?"

"I'm trying to. Give me a chance." He patted his pockets, looking for a cigarette. "Well, Toni, we've been talking a lot, your mother and me."

"Because of you," her mother put in. "Because of everything with you, Toni."

"Violet, do you want me to—"

"No, you talk, Hal. It's your show. Go ahead." Her mother ran water into the teakettle. "I won't interrupt."

Her father stared at the cigarette that he held between his fingers. "I want to explain something. A long time ago your mother and I had problems. You know something about that. The way I see it, I mean, the way we both see it, is that we had our problems, but we never, uh, settled them." He spoke slowly. "We decided to go on. We wanted you to grow up in a house with two parents. That was the main thing."

"She knows that," Toni's mother said. "I've talked to her about it. I told her that."

Her father frowned. "When you brought all that stuff up about the hitting and the fights, I didn't want to remember it. I didn't want to talk about it. The hitting, especially that. We haven't talked about those things for a long time."

"For forever," her mother said dryly. She sat down. "When I was pregnant with you, your father and I made an agreement. We promised each other to forget the bad stuff, to put it behind us. Things had gotten out of hand. I said we were going to control ourselves, and your father agreed. The hitting . . . I knew that was never going to happen again. It never did."

Toni's father nodded.

Toni stared from one to the other. Her cheeks were burning, there was a clatter in her chest. "What are you saying to me? What are you telling me? That it doesn't matter that he hit you?"

"Ahh, no," her mother said. "It matters. It's there. There's nothing we can do about that, but it also matters that we didn't let it ruin our lives. We stopped it. It ended. We went on with our lives, with *your* life. Most of all we both wanted to make something good for you. We stayed together for you."

"I know," Toni said. "I've heard that before."

Her father turned his head and blew out a mouthful of smoke. "Listen, you seem to have an idea that—Listen! It wasn't like being in prison. There was something there, there was more than duty or, or habit, or doing the right thing."

"We're not just saying this in an offhand way," her mother said. "We want you to know . . . we—we have feelings—" Her mother faltered, and her eyes filled. "What . . . what do you think is going to happen when you go to college? That's not so far away. You think we're going to fall apart? That we'll just walk away from each other? No, there is affection here, Toni, there is something here between your father and me." Her mother wiped her eyes. "There always has been."

"And now it's going to be better," her father said.

"Because of you," her mother said. She reached for Toni's hand. "It's opened things up and we're talking. I mean, really talking, more than we have in a long time. Isn't that strange?"

Her father put his hand over her mother's hand. "Do you understand?" he said to Toni. "Do you understand what we're trying to tell you?"

Toni's father had begun walking every morning on the towpath bordering the canal. "I'm up to a mile and a quarter," he said one morning at the table. "How about that, Toni?"

She was reading the newspaper. "Good."

He tapped the paper, waited until she looked up, then took out a cigarette and shredded it over a plate. "My last one," he said. "That's it. I'm done. Right, Violet?"

Toni's mother sat down with a cup of coffee. "Your father's joined a stop-smoking group."

They both watched her.

"Does my daughter have anything to say to that?" her father said.

"Congratulations," Toni said.

"And that's it?"

"Good for you, Dad," she said softly.

Julie's parents went on a trip to Niagara Falls. "To rediscover their romance," Julie drawled on the way to school. He father had returned two days ago. "And my mother let him into her life again, as cool as you please. Like he went to the store for a loaf of bread. Five months ago."

"She wasn't even mad?" Toni said.

"Jerrine? Not her. She said, 'Oh, I'm all over that.' Great. I am never going to let a man walk over me. And you better not, either."

"L.R. is not the type to walk over a person."

"Who's talking about L.R.?" Julie said. "I'm talking about the future, about real life."

"This *is* my real life, Julie."

Julie grunted. "Mine begins in four years."

Toni shifted her books from one arm to the other. "Jul, what if my friendship with L.R. escalates?"

"Meaning what?"

Toni looked up at the sky. "We kissed."

"You kissed?"

She nodded.

"You really did? When?"

"The movies, yesterday."

"How was it?"

"Good movie, you should see it."

"Thanks a lot. Now tell me, how was it?"

"I probably shouldn't talk about it."

"Yes, you should."

"It was nice. I mean, it was *nice,* Julie."

"Nice?"

"*Nice.*"

"Wet?"

"I didn't notice."

"You did too."

"It was a little smooshy."

"What's smooshy? It sounds like he smashed his mouth against yours. Did he stick his tongue in, too, or is he too polite?"

"Don't ask so many questions."

"Oh! So he did."

A little later, just before they crossed the street to the school, Toni said, "Julie, I want to ask you something. Is it really okay with you about me and L.R.?"

Julie shrugged. "He's yours, darling."

"But you were in love with him."

"I needed some excitement in my life." Julie smiled a little. "It was easy to be in love when I didn't actually know him. It was fun," she said.

How different they were, Tony thought. Of course, they always had been, but now it was so clear to her. So were some other things. How she'd always clung to Julie, thinking that Julie was the strong one. A little sadness pierced her. Their friendship had changed. It would always be there, but on a different basis. It was as if they'd been walking along side by side, and suddenly, without meaning to, she'd gone ahead of Julie.

Julie hit Toni on the arm. Hard. "Hey!" Toni said, and she hit Julie back, just as hard. "What's your problem?" she said.

"I'm envious," Julie said with a tiny smile. "I hate it that you've been kissed before me. I always thought I'd be first."

"So did I," Toni said wonderingly.

Toni woke up early. She reached for the glass cat and rested it against her eyelids. Its cool weight always brought back that day when she and her father had driven to the glass factory in Corning: the two of them together; the long, sloping road past the lake; the green hills. They'd stopped for lunch in a diner. She'd eaten a cheese sandwich and the best rice pudding she'd ever had.

Downstairs, she heard her father moving around in the kitchen. The cat was pink in a certain light, blue in others. Like music, almost. She remembered the steel drummer in the park in New York saying, "The heart must be clear for the music," and how that had impressed her. She hadn't understood it exactly, she still didn't completely . . . but it seemed like something that she should remember.

She got out of bed and went downstairs. Her father was looking out the window, a cup in his hand. He turned, hearing her. "You're up early."

She stood next to him, looking out the window, too. "What's the weather report?"

"Cloudy, but it might clear. One of those nice but not perfect days." He put bread in the toaster. "Can I make you something?"

She shook her head. "Are you walking this morning?" He nodded, and she said, "How do you feel about company?"

He looked at her, took the bread out of the toaster, and put it on a plate. Then he said, "Some questions don't have to be asked."

"I'll just go change, then," she said, and she started up the stairs. "Wait for me, will you?"

NORMA FOX MAZER grew up in Glens Falls, New York, in the foothills of the Adirondack Mountains. She has been writing all her life and is the author of many acclaimed books for young readers, including the Avon Flare titles *After the Rain* (a 1988 Newbery Honor Book and ALA Best Book for Young Adults); *Taking Terri Mueller* (winner of the 1981 Edgar Award for Best Juvenile Mystery); *Downtown* and *Silver* (both ALA Best Books for Young Adults); and *Mrs. Fish, Ape, and Me, the Dump Queen*. Ms. Mazer and her husband, novelist Harry Mazer, currently make their home in the Pompey Hills of central New York State.